An Isaac Smith Mystery

# Promise
# to a
# Dead Man

## Part One

## *By L. Z. Smith*

*The facade of the Chinese ... is smooth and has un-varying features. It seems as if nothing could ruffle its surface. It is a face that communicates that it is hiding something about which we know nothing and never will.*

*Ryszard Kapusinski*
*Travels with Herodotus*

*Copyright © 2011 by Lincoln Smith*
*ISBN#13-9780985209711*
*Library of Congress Card Number:TXu1-763-327*

*Global Talent Agency, LLC*
*a wholly owned subsidary of Global Artist Agency, LLC.*
*Burbank, California*

*Cover by Marta*

Local4Publishing
Localfourpublishing@gmail.com

# CHAPTER ONE

My short abstention from Jack Daniels and Lucky Strikes came to an abrupt halt. A shrink would probably have diagnosed me manic depressive. It had been several years since my junket into sex, violence, and corruption, and now my job had become mundane and my life boring. My career as head of a small Oakland culinary union ended when I resigned six months after my appointment—politics and book-keeping just didn't cut it. I was a union business agent and I liked it that way. I had been appointed president of the Local after my predecessor and his gang of thugs had been busted for dealing coke out of the union hall. How he ever got elected in the first place still baffled me. But it was Oakland and shit happens

What ever made me think being a representative of working people would help change the world? Whatever it was that made my parents believe in the revolution of the proletariat all their lives had become lost in the haze of history and the collapse the Soviet Union. Was it all bullshit?

Being a Business Agent at Culinary Local 4 was a thankless and frustrating job; the decline of union joints, thanks to competition from the non-union restaurants that sprang up like weeds everywhere and was making my job seem futile. I had considered quitting the union business altogether. But that all changed one uncharacteristically hot day in June of 1991 when l was called on to defend an old Chinese bartender at the Hyatt Regency who had been fired on trumped up charges. Little did I know at the time that I would be dragged into an international conspiracy that went far beyond my pay grade.

Management had been lying to get rid of him for years. But Peter Wu was a model employee; showed up on time, never took a day off, and mixed a damn good martini. They finally cooked up a plan and accused him of stealing; something they knew Peter Wu would never do.

I scanned the grievance board members faces. It was the usual; the three well-dressed members on the employer's side, sitting upright with their self-righteous smiles; the union's side, also self righteous, but indignant and arrogant and casual in attire.

Like most Asians I couldn't tell how old Peter was. He was tall for being Chinese and the creases that lined his face couldn't have been any more perfectly set had they been put there by a makeup artist. He slicked back his graying black hair exposing a high forehead, not unlike pictures I had seen of Mao Tse-tung, and he spoke in a broken English. I had known him for a long time. He was a humble man and, to my mind, too polite, as if he was always trying to please. It was a trait I found somewhat irritating and endearing at the same time. You just couldn't help but like Peter Wu.

At the head of the long conference table sat Phyllis Wills,

the hotels' personnel director. I'd know Phyllis for many years. She was one of those turn coats; learning her trade as a union representative and then switched to the bosses' side. Now she was a union hater, and she especially hated me.

Mr. Wu sat alongside me. I had no idea how long he had been in the country or if he was even legal, but then that's not the union's business. I was his Business Agent and it was my job to represent the members of Culinary Local 4 when they get into a jam with their boss, not check their legal status. Most of them worked hard, paid their dues, and were generally good union members Peter I especially liked. He attended every union meeting he could, never saying a thing, just listening. He walked every union called picket line when he wasn't scheduled to work. For some reason he considered me a friend, even inviting me to his house for dinner to meet his niece. I always found an excuse not to go. Peter deserved the best representation I could give him.

Phyllis had just finished up her side of the case. Her first witness was the young debonair black bar manager, Manny Foster, in his starched white shirt, red power tie and Armani sport jacket. His testimony amounted to; there was money missing and Mr. Wu was the only one who could have taken it. No proof, just "Wu took it."

Her second witness, the head of security, had nothing at all to do with the incident. He was called in simply to offer his "expert" testimony about how most cases of stealing by employees occurred and that Mr. Wu fit the profile despite the fact there was no evidence at all. But he was impressive and I could see management's side of the table nodding their heads like a bunch of bobble head dolls in the back of a Tijuana taxi.

It was my turn to present the union' side; I knew it was an exercise in futility. Grievance boards usually were. The outcome was almost certain to be a stale mate. The bosses' people would uphold the termination. The Union in most cases voted to overturn it unless the employee really fucked up. Most Business Agents won't take a case to a board unless they feel sure the termination was without merit. But the union contract called for a grievance procedure and the board was the last step before arbitration. The notes that both sides took could be a major factor in presenting the case to an arbitrator.

I believe one could safely say the hotel wanted to get rid of Mr. Wu because an older Chinese bartender, even one on the morning shift, doesn't fit into their idea of what a cocktail lounge in a four star hotel should look like. I am sure Mr. Foster would prefer to hire a young attractive woman more in keeping with the yuppie image the hotel was trying to nurture. Besides that, the employer offered no concrete evidence that Mr. Wu stole anything, I said.

"And as for their expert witness, well, let me tell you a little story my uncle once told me," I said.

Phyllis jumped out of her chair, banging the table with her fist. "Mr. Smith, we are not interested in hearing your stories."

"Excuse me, Ms. Wills, but you had your turn. Now it's the union's turn."

She sat back in her chair and folded her arms in disgust and resignation.

"As I was saying, there were four rabbis who used to argue theology together, and three were always in accord against the fourth. One day, the odd rabbi out, after losing three to one again, decided to appeal to a higher authority.

"'Oh, God!' he cried. 'I know in my heart that I am right and they are wrong! Please give a sign to prove it to them!'

"It was a beautiful, sunny day. As soon as the rabbi finished his prayer, a storm cloud moved across the sky above the four rabbis. It rumbled once and dissolved.

"'A sign from God! You see, I am right! I knew it!' the rabbi said. But the other three disagreed, pointing out that storm clouds often form on hot days.

"So the rabbi prayed again. 'O, God, I need a bigger sign to show that I am right and they are wrong. So please, God, a bigger sign!' This time four storm clouds appeared, rushed toward each other to form one big cloud, and a bolt of lightning slammed into a tree on a nearby hill.

"'You see? God agrees. I am right!' cried the rabbi, but his friends insisted that a thunder storm on a hot day was quite natural.

"The rabbi was getting ready to ask for a very, very big sign, but just as he said, 'O. God ...,' the sky turned pitch-black, the earth shook, and a deep, booming voice intoned,

"'HEEEEEEEE'S RIIIIGHT!'"

"The rabbi put his hands on his hips, turned to the other three, and said, 'Well?'

"'So,' shrugged one of the other rabbis, 'now it's three to two.'"

There was a moment of silence, and then two of the board members from the union laughed out loud. The third just leaned back in her chair and smiled smuugle. The three on the employer's side, who had been busy scribbling notes on their yellow legal pads, sat with bewildered looks on their faces. Phyllis threw her pencil down on the table and stormed out of the conference room to her adjoining office and slammed the door.

"And that's my response to your so-called expert witness," I said. "Now I will ask Mr. Wu a couple of questions." I turned to Wu who was sitting patiently with his head down and his hands clasped between his knees. "Mr. Wu, how long have you worked for the Hyatt?"

"Since hotel open, long time," Wu stammered.

Have you ever taken money from the hotel?"

"No, Wu no steal," he answered.

"Without supporting evidence this turns out to be Mr. Wu's word against Mr. Foster's," I said. "There is no just cause for termination. Mr. Wu should be reinstated with full back pay."

I picked up my legal pad, nodded for Wu to come with me, and we walked out into the cavernous bowels of the hotel basement.

People were hurrying around in all directions. The basement opened onto the loading dock where men and women in cook's jackets were inspecting food deliveries and porters carted boxes on hand trucks heading toward the large service elevators. Waiters were busily clasping on bow ties and buttoning up white shirts before picking up their jackets which were hung out in front of the in-house laundry, cleaned and starched until they were like cardboard. It all seemed like chaos, except that everyone knew exactly what their job was and how to do it with the professionalism and efficiency that goes unseen by hotel guests.

"They are good workers," Wu commented. "In China they would be treated with respect."

"That's why we have unions," I said.

"In China the union and managers work as one in harmony. It makes for better job."

We started walking toward the stairs leading down into the rear parking lot.

"That proverb you told, about the four rabbis..." Wu said.

"Yeah, it's a story my uncle used to tell me when I was a kid."

"That is very much like a Chinese proverb we were taught when young," Wu said. "We have much in common."

"Sure, Jews and Chinese." I said skeptically.

"So I return to work tomorrow?"

"No Peter. We will have to go to arbitration first. It will take a couple of months."

"How Wu to live? I have niece goes to university. I need support her"

"I'll see if I can get you some work through the hiring hall."

"Surely this arbitration will put me back to work."

"It's likely," I said, not wanting to tell him that truth and right aren't always the criteria for an arbitrator's decision. Most of them liked to split up their decisions between the employer's side and the union's. They had to keep both sides happy if they wanted to keep getting jobs, and arbitrators charged an arm and a leg for their service. They were lawyers after all.

Just then someone called out to me. I turned and saw a young white guy in a waiter's uniform. I recognized him. He was a chronic complainer, only his beef was always with either the union, or a fellow employee, or both. But I couldn't ignore him.

"Excuse me, Peter," I apologized. "I'll have to take care of this. Meet me back at the union hall in about an hour and we'll go over your case."

"Yes sir, Mr. Smitty. An hour."

And I knew he'd be on time to the minute. Wu continued on toward the back stairs as I turned to talk to Todd, the young waiter, when several loud pops rang out, echoing and reverberating through the vast basement and sending people scurrying and ducking for cover. I swung around in the direction of the sound in time to see Wu folding up like a collapsing building, and a man running down the steps where he disappeared into the parking lot.

I ran over to where Wu was lying on his back on the cold concrete floor as a pool of red began to spread around him. His eyes, which were no more than two slashes below bushy black and silver eye brows, stared up at me.

"Peter, are you ok?" I said, immediately feeling like an ass because it was obvious he wasn't.

He grabbed hold of my hand as I lifted his head up. I heard shouts in the background but they all seemed far away as Wu grabbed hold of my wrist, squeezed my hand tightly as if it was the only thing keeping the life from flowing out of him.

"Smitty, you must take care of my niece, Mei-ling. They will be after her." His voice was chocked and weak, but insistent.

"What, who will be after her?" I said, but he grabbed hold of me tighter with amazing strength.

"You must take care of her," he insisted. "There's no one else I can trust. You are my business agent. You must help me. You must promise."

It suddenly occurred to me that he had totally lost his accent.

"Swear, Smitty, so I can go to my ancestors with peace of mind."

"OK, I'll take care of her Wu."

"Swear to me,"

"I swear," I said.

Then Wu closed his eyes and I felt his grip on me loosen. His hand fell to his chest. I gentle laid his head on the cold ground. It was then I realized we were surrounded by people, eyes staring down at the limp body of the Chinese bartender. Several women were crying.

"Alright, get back everyone. Move aside. Let me through."

It was the harsh authoritarian voice of the Personnel Director who pushed herself through the crowd, followed by an entourage of managers and the head of security that had been at the board hearing.

"What the hell's going on here, Isaac?" Then she saw what had happened. "Isaac, is that Mr. Wu? Oh god, this is terrible. What happened?"

I looked around at the staring faces.

"For Christ's sake, someone get a sheet or something to cover him up," I said.

Then I heard one of the manager's remark, "I guess this takes care of the grievance."

"Shut up," Phyllis said, and I thought that perhaps I had misjudged her.

Someone handed me a freshly folded and starched white

table cloth they must have gotten from the laundry. Another pair of hands helped me open it and spread it over the dead bartender as sirens screamed into the parking lot.

"What are you doing Isaac, that's hotel property!"

Phyllis' voice rose sharply, and my momentary feeling of good will toward her evaporated.

""Fuck you, Phyllis," I said and then pushed myself past her and walked away.

I heard her irritating voice in the back ground. "OK people, get back to work. We have a hotel to run...."

* * *

# CHAPTER 2

I stopped at the first liquor store I came to and bought a pint of Jack Daniels and a pack of Luckys, and then headed for my apartment on Lake Merritt, trying to shake the dead stare of Peter Wu that only the Jack could chase away

The empty apartment added to my depression even though I hadn't been staying there much. I spent a lot of my nights on the forty-two foot Rough Water I kept in the Emeryville Marina. I had bought it with insurance dough from my old 32 foot Owens that had burned to the water line in '89. The apartment on Lakeshore I inherited from a lady friend after she ran off to Modesto to open a bar with an old flame.

I now shared the apartment with a young Black woman whose name had been Jasmine when I first met her. She was a hooker working out of the Hyatt Hotel at the time, and hung out at my pal Eddy's Ringside bar down the street from the

Tribune building. She was not only beautiful, but intelligent and independent. She had plans for her future and they didn't include selling her body on the street. She liked me because I respected her, and would never pay her for sex, not that I didn't want to, but because it was against my principles. She respected that and we became good friends.

Now she was going to Cal State full time studying to be a social worker. She had practiced the world's oldest profession to make enough money to support her daughter and grandmother in a small house in South Berkeley. When her Grandmother died I convinced her to give up the life and moved her in with me.

In the beginning we were like young lovers. I got her a part-time gig working as a counselor for sex workers through my political connections at City Hall. But soon her energy focused in on her daughter, Chanel, and her studies, and the passion faded. I started to believe her lovemaking had been more out of gratitude, but we reMeined good friends, and she continued to share her bed, making love to me on occasion. That's when I started spending more time on my boat in Emeryville, realizing that the sex had been a huge middle aged ego trip. Now she and Chanel were like the only family I had.

Recently she and her daughter had gone to care for her ailing aunt who lived on a farm in Arkansas, and my loneliness closed in further after a brief phone call: The aunt was worse and Adede, her real name although I had taken to calling her Dede, didn't know when they would return. The rest of that day melted into a haze of cigarette smoke and booze.

When I woke up the next morning there were two empty pint bottles of Jack Daniels on the floor and my head was inhabited by a jack hammer. The phone was ranging in my ears. I tossed aside Chanel's stuffed panda bear that had become my pillow. Ted was on the other end of the phone line yelling. He was the top crime reporter for the *Oakland Tribune* and a close friend. He was doing a story on the murder at the Hyatt, and why the fuck hadn't I called him, his best friend, to tell him what had happened. I managed to calm him down and made arrangements to meet for dinner that evening. I fumbled around for a Lucky after hanging up, and the first drag made my head swim. It was already eight and the sun streamed through the window.

A hot shower and a cup of reheated coffee cleared my head; I was out the door heading to the Lake Merritt Restaurant for a newspaper and more coffee. It looked like it would be a nice day. The morning sun sparkled off the lake as early morning joggers ran in endless circles, and old people sat on benches watching them while reading the *Tribune*; probably a story by Ted about the mysterious gangland style murder of an old Chinese bartender in front of dozens of witnesses in the basement of the city's only major hotel.

It was nearly ten by the time I finished my coffee and *Trib*. I was right about the story in the paper; boiler plate crime reporting: The 48th homicide in Oakland for the Year; no leads, witnesses said the killer wore a black ski mask over his face and ran off before anyone knew what happened, probably gang related....etc. etc.

The restaurant and bakery were not the same since my friend Flo had retired and I had to pay my own tab. I decided to walk to Chinatown and look in on Peter Wu's niece. It would take about a half an hour, but it was a good morning for a walk. The address I got from Peter's file was on Jefferson Street in the heart of Chinatown.

Unlike San Francisco's large Chinatown which was like a Disneyland for tourists—the idea of some prominent Chinese business men after the earth quake in '06 had destroyed the city—Oakland's Chinatown was exclusively for the Chinese and Asian community; six square blocks of small restaurants, bakeries, herb and acupuncture practitioners, markets with greasy brown ducks hanging by their necks in the window and piles of neatly stacked vegetables with exotic names on display

16

to be picked over by old Chinese woman. Mornings were especially busy, with delivery trucks of every size, double parked and clogging up the narrow one way streets. I stopped for a moment to peer into large wood barrels being unloaded by two burly white guys with cigarettes hanging from their lips. Inside were large frogs and turtles piled neatly on top of each other, quietly waiting to be slaughtered, sold and turned into stew or soup.

Peter's house wasn't hard to find. A crowd of people stood in front of it. Bouquets of flowers clogged the staircase. I pushed my way toward the front of the crowd that had spilled into the streets. Suddenly a black limo flying the flags of The People's Republic of China, know by most folks as "Red China", blew its horn as a couple of cops cleared a path to the curb in front on the stair case. Apparently Pete Wu was more than just a bartender in Chinatown. A chauffeur jumped out and ran to the back door. Two men in black suits and black fedoras stepped out. One carried a bouquet of red roses; the other a large stuffed panda bear. They laid them on the stairs and then proceeded to the front door. They were greeted by a woman with a slight bow. She was striking, dressed in black with a black veil covering her face. The dress clung to a trim body and one shapely leg wrapped in black nylon was exposed to the thigh from the slits up the side. This was Peter's niece the college student?

"Smitty...." I heard a voice call, but all I saw was a sea of yellow faces and dark almond shaped eyes. "Smitty, over here." It was Johnny Wong, the bartender at the Oaks Club waving at me, and then all the faces took shape around me: An old woman clutching a crucifix with tears streaming down her wrinkled yellow skin, a middle aged couple holding hands and bowing their heads, others with two hands closed together in Buddhist prayer.....

"Smitty, what the hell you doing here?" Johnny Wong asked as he pushed his way through the crowd.

"Johnny, I could ask you the same thing."

"Me, I come to pay my respects."

"You knew Peter Wu?"

"Smitty, be serious. There are two Chinese bartenders in the union...well, now there's one, me. Of course I knew Peter. Hell, everyone in Chinatown knew Peter Wu. Come on, my cousin runs a small bakery around the corner. I'll buy you a cup of coffee and we can talk."

Johnny's cousin's bakery was a hole in the wall, with enough window space to display a selection of pork buns and two small tables.

"I know it don't look like much but my cousin sells five hundred to a thousand pork bows out of here a day. His wife and mother-in- law do all the work. Low over head, big profit," Johnny said sitting at one of the tables.

Johnny's father was a big shot in Chinatown; owner of the Wong Oriental Foods Distribution Company, and who knows what else. Johnny says he didn't like working in the business and became a bartender instead. But, according to the Chinese cooks at the Oaks, his father planted him in the card club after it introduced Pai Gow, putting it in direct competition with the Triangle Card Room across the street on San Pablo Avenue in Emeryville, the small town between Oakland and Berkeley along the waterfront. Old man Wong, they said, was part owner of the Triangle Card Room that had catered primarily to Chinese gamblers. Rumor had it that it was a front for opium smuggling and God knows what else. But the Triangle operated outside of Chinatown and the cops were constantly raiding it. Aside from all that, Johnny was a good union man, and had become a friend over the years.

"Coffee?" he asked as I squeezed into the chair opposite him. "And you gotta try the pork bow. I recommend the steamed ones, best in Chinatown."

'Sure."

Johnny called over to the woman behind the counter in Chinese. Two cups of steaming coffee appeared at the table.

"So you were at the hotel when Peter was shot?" he said.

"Me and a hundred hotel workers."

"Yeah, but Peter died in your arms."

"How do you know all that, Johnny?" I asked.

"My cousin, he works in the Hotel laundry. He was there."

"Say, is there anyone in Chinatown that's not your cousin?"

"Big Family, us Wongs," he laughed.

"So Johnny, why the fuck would anyone want to shot down old Peter?"

He shrugged and poured some sugar into his coffee, almost like he was ignoring my question. Then he looked up and stared at me for a moment. "Smitty, did he say something to you before he died?"

I took a sip of my coffee. "Well, he said something about his niece, like she could be in danger too. What do you suppose he meant by that?"

"Well Smitty, me personally, I didn't know what Peter Wu was into around Chinatown; just that he was well respected. But after seeing the Consulate here, well, those guys don't venture into Oakland often. They gotta get State Department clearance to leave San Francisco, so who knows what our Peter was in to." He called to the woman behind the counter again and said something in Chinese to her. Then back to me, "If you're worried about his niece, you'd best come back tomorrow. You'll never get in to see her today."

The woman brought over a pink box, neatly tied with string.

"Here," Johnny said. "You bring her these in the morning. It's custom to bring some food. You come see me anytime. Maybe I can help you out. Be careful around Chinatown, Smitty. Never know what's going on."

\* \* \*

# CHAPTER 3

I was anxious to meet with Ted. I got back to the apartment and lay down. I must have slept because it was four in the afternoon when I woke up starving.

Three years before, Ted had exposed an extortion racket in Chinatown after an extensive investigation for the *Tribune*. I thought he might be able to give me some information on why someone would shoot an old Chinese bartender in broad daylight at the Hyatt Hotel.

Ted and I had history, dating back to the days when he was a reporter for the UC Berkeley newspaper, *The Daily Californian*, and I was bartending a small joint near campus. He had stumbled into the bar after being hit over the head by a cop's baton during the massive so-called Peoples' Park demonstrations in the sixties.

That was when the governor had called out the National Guard to break the back of the demonstrators. All he accomplished was a lot of broken heads, two dead students and the undying hatred of thousands of Berkeley students and residents.

The Golden Pagoda was an old joint that had seen better days. I had picked it because it was close to the Lake. I could walk there, and it wasn't in Chinatown. After talking with Johnny I was getting a little paranoid.

A faded newspaper article in the window of the Pagoda bragged how it was the first major Chinese restaurant to open outside of Chinatown, along with a picture that dated back to the earlier part of the century.

Ted hadn't showed yet so I let myself be seated at a small window table with a white carnation in a plastic vase holding down a bright red table cloth. A waiter, who had probably been there since the restaurant opened, greeted me with a frozen frown that seemed painted on his pale yellow face.

"You want cocktail?" he said in English that probably hadn't improved since he first hit the immigration center on Angel Island.

"I guess I'll have a Tsingtao and you can bring a dry martini for my friend whose coming. I'll order now."

Ted showed up by the time I was ready for another beer.

"Well, I suppose you want to know about yesterday," I said as he sat down, avoiding small talk.

"Well, yes, that would be nice. You got a front row seat to murder at the Hyatt. Do you call me; your best friend who you know is an award winning crime reporter?"

"I'm sorry, Ted, but don't be a prick about it. It's not every day I have a man die in my arms. I was pretty shook up."

"Oh, all right. But next time some homicide victim dies in your arms give me call, would you?

"Let's hope this was the last time. So, what do you know?"

"Other then what was in the paper today, I haven't turned in my full story yet, just in case you have anything I don't know."

"Tsingtao." The old Chinese waiter poured out a half a glass and placed the bottle in front of me while retrieving the empty. "And a martini for the gentleman." He set a shiny glass of clear liquid sporting two small green olives on the end of an umbrella toothpick in front of Ted.

"Thanks," I said, but the old man had already drifted off. "There's really nothing to tell," I said, turning to Ted. "I was there with Peter at a grievance board. He had been fired. We finished and went out into the basement. I went to talk to another member and someone shot him. That's it"

"Why was he fired?"

"Huh, what difference does that make?"

"You're right. Well, it's nothing I don't already know. But still, you could have called me."

"I don't get it, Ted. Why would anyone want to gun down a harmless old Chinese bartender? It doesn't make sense. I mean, I could see if he had been shot in a street robbery, but this was like a gangland hit."

"Well, maybe not," Ted said just as our waiter brought two steaming plates of food, carefully set them down and then walked off. Ted's eyes followed the old man. "You know what they say about Chinatown; nothing is as it seems. Behind the curio shops, restaurants and markets lies an entire world hidden from us round eyes."

Ted billed himself an expert on Chinatown, "Stop talking riddles and tell me what you know," I said, cutting him off mid-sentence.

"So, like the good reporter that I am, I was as puzzled as you. I called a friend of mine at Immigration and asked him to run a check on your Peter Wu the bartender.

"And?"

"Well, it seems his real name is Ching-Shu Wu, Captain Ching–Shu Wu. He was an intelligence officer in the PLA during the Korean War.

"PLA?"

"People's Liberation Army, also referred to as the Red Army. After the war he was stationed in Guanzhu City where he became head of Internal Security. According to the FBI's report on him your friend Wu was headed up in the party hierarchy. But when Mao proclaimed the Cultural Revolution he dropped out of sight. All they know after that was the next time he was heard from was when he turned up in San Francisco in 1974 seeking political asylum."

"Jesus. You sure it's the same Peter Wu?"

"Well, my source is pretty reliable," Ted said with that reporter's authority that always bugged the shit out of me. "Let's eat."

We both fell silent. I watched as Ted spooned heaps of the usual shrimp in garlic sauce and chicken Chow Mien onto his plate. I had suddenly lost my appetite. Old Peter Wu an officer in the Chinese Red Army, gunned down in broad daylight?

"Ted, do me a favor and don't put that in your story...not yet at least."

He looked up, Chow Mien noodles hanging from his mouth.

"What? Why not?"

"I have my reasons. A girl's life might depend on it."

"What the fuck are you talking about?"

"Just don't print that information. I'll give you all the details when I know what's going on. It could be a big story."

"Hmmm, I don't know. If I don't print it the *Chronicle* or *Examiner* might beat me to it. They already got reporters nosing around. Hell, any good reporter would want to find out why someone went through all the trouble to murder your poor old bartender in broad daylight. Gotta be a story there somewhere, don't you think?"

"Well, I wish you'd hold it for a couple of days."

"It'll be old news in a couple of days, Smitty. But I'll think about it."

"Thanks." I said, knowing Ted could no more hold back on a story like this than I could not go see Peter's niece."

Ted ran a napkin over is mouth and gulped down the rest of his Martini. "Well, I gotta run."

He stood up and walked out, leaving me with the tab. He was good at that.

\* \* \*

# CHAPTER 4

The flowers from the day before were gone. The front steps empty. The sun was peeking over the East Bay hills. I hadn't been able to sleep in anticipation of my meeting with Mei-ling Wu.

The woman who came to the door was not what I expected when I thought of a college girl. She was a handsome woman, with high cheek bones, full lips and large green almond eyes, all wrapped in a pink embroidered silk dressing gown.

"Can I help you? I told the police everything I know yesterday."

"I'm not a cop," I said. "My name is Isaac Smith. I was your uncle's union representative."

"Smitty?"

"Yes, that's what people call me."

"Yes, my uncle had spoken of you often," she said, removing the chain lock and opening the door. "Please come in. I'll fix some tea"

"Thanks."

She led me into a small sitting room overlooking the street. It was furnished part Asian, part American contemporary; an odd mixture, but appropriate I thought.

"Please make yourself comfortable while I fix some tea, or would you prefer coffee?"

"Tea is fine."

I couldn't help but admire the flowery robe that revealed her shapely legs and trim little body. She pulled the robe tight around her, so that it pressed against her small breasts, whose erect nipples pressed hard against the fine pink silk material. What an asshole. I had come to offer my condolences and all I could think of was the woman's body.

"Oh, here," I said clumsily, holding out the little pink box with the pork buns. "I was told it was custom to bring these when visiting."

She smiled and opened the box and set it on the coffee table. "I will be right back. Please make yourself comfortable."

She disappeared down a long hallway.

The perfume of the dozens of flower bouquets filled the air. On a corner table was the large stuffed panda I had seen the Chinese Consul present her. I wondered its significance. There was a small envelope with Chinese writing. I don't know why, but I took it and slipped it into my pocket.

I looked around. The walls were neatly decorated with Chinese prints and framed pictures and documents. I noticed several degrees from UC Berkeley in Asian studies alongside some official looking scrolls in Chinese. There were some faded photographs with distinguished looking Chinese men and women and one of a young man in a military uniform. I assumed it was Peter.

Mei-ling returned with a tray holding a teapot and two cups, much like the kind you get in a Chinese restaurant, only more elaborate. She set it down on the small coffee table next to the pink box of pork buns, and sat next to me on the love seat. I could feel the warmth that radiated from her.

"I'm sorry I missed the funeral," I said rather clumsily. "What funeral home is he at?"

She carefully poured out two cups of steaming tea.

"Oh, my uncle's reMeins are on the way back to China to be buried with our ancestors. The Chinese consulate was very helpful in making the arrangements."

I took a sip of the hot tea. "Yes, I saw them here yesterday. I had no idea Peter was such an important man."

"He was well respected in the Chinese community, Mr. Smith."

"Please, call me Smitty."

"If you like."

"Listen Miss Wu, let me be frank. Your uncle died in my arms, and his last words were to make me promise to watch over you; that you were in some kind of danger. What do you suppose he meant by that?"

She lifted her tea cup to her mouth. Her green eyes looked into mine as she sipped; the steam rose around her face. "Why, I don't know what you mean."

She put down her cup and put her warm hand on mine. I couldn't help but be attracted to her.

"I assure you, Mr. Smith..."

"Smitty."

"Smitty. I don't need watching over although I appreciate your concern."

I put my hand over hers and she didn't resist. "Miss Wu..."

"Mei."

"Mei. Your uncle's last wish was for me to keep you safe. I don't know why he asked that of me, but when a dying man asks you to do something, well; you're supposed to do it."

She gave me a sad smile and put her other hand over mine. "Smitty, you are a very sweet man. But I assure you I will be fine."

Then she leaned over and gentle kissed my cheek. I was completely surprised.

"Would you mind if I came back and checked up on you this afternoon. No matter what you say, I am still concerned." The words seemed wooden and clumsy as they came out. I stood up to leave. She rose with me, our hands still clasped.

"You haven't touched your tea."

"I have to go to work."

She walked me to the door, still holding my hand.

"Come for dinner, around six," she said opening the door.

"I would like that."

Then she surprised me again by leaning in and kissing me on the mouth. Her lips were soft and velvety and she smelled of gardenias. Her body pressed slightly against mine and I felt a stirring of passion. Then I was out on the street.

\* \* \*

# CHAPTER 5

The morning sun hit my eyes as I stepped out onto the street. I walked down the stairs from the house and headed north on Jefferson when I noticed a Black Toyota sports car with a Asian man watching me from behind a pair of Ray-Ban sunglasses. I gave him a "who the fuck are you" look and then continued to walk. I stopped at the corner and watched. The Toyota speed off down the street.

I headed down to Broadway to DeLaurers, the oldest establishment in downtown Oakland. DeLauers sells cigarettes, cigars, magazines on every subject imaginable, and newspapers from all over the world. As I stood in line for a pack of Luckys a headline in the L.A. Times caught my eye: **"27 *Chinese immigrants found dead in freight container."*** Usually a headline like that wouldn't faze me, just another tragedy in a tragic world. But now, because of a dead Chinese bartender and his very alive niece, it seemed my life was to become intimately entangled in things Chinese. I remembered the last time I had ventured into that unknown world it had almost cost me my life. A chill went down my spine. I picked up the paper and bought it along with the cigarettes.

Back out on the street I made my way up Broadway to where the Cathedral Building sliced into it like a gothic wedge, sending it forking off to the right while Telegraph Avenue veered to the left. The beautiful Gothic building demarcated where Up Town Oakland began. Now its magnificence was made almost comical by the Popeye's Fried Chicken restaurant on the ground floor; a mocking reminder of how far the city had deteriorated over the years. I walked on, past the cheap wig and jewelry shops spaced between chained up store fronts, and past the once majestic Fox Theater, now boarded up and falling into decay while politicians and developers argued over whether or not to restore it. Another block and past the Emporium, the last of the great department stores in Oakland on the corner of Telegraph and Fourteenth. West on Nineteenth the Union hall sat like a cement block fortress. Built by the Waitress' Union in the heyday '50s when its membership was close to ten thousand, it was taken over when the International Union merged them in with the Cooks' and the Bartenders' locals. The honest leadership was usurped by a shady union hood exported from the East Coast. It was downhill from there on, until the membership shrank to a little more than 3000 and leveled off, and the once rich union had been looted of every dime.

Inside the glass doors and into the foyer I was greeted by Marta from the dispatch window. She was new and wasn't the most friendly woman, but she was efficient and bilingual, and since many of our job calls were for dish washers or prep cooks who didn't speak English, she was indispensable. But I missed Lil, the previous dispatcher who had retired a year before.

"Smitty, gotta couple of messages for you." She handed me the pink "while you were out" slips. No mention of Peter Wu or how I felt. She was all business.

The door buzzed me into the inner sanctum of the hall with partitioned offices and a huge wall safe which once held bushels of money and other valuables, but now acted as a kind of storage

30

area. I glanced at the notes. One from Ted: "Urgent I see you. Call", and one from Mei-ling: "Thanks for coming by. I look forward to tonight".

I went into my cramped office and called Ted. He didn't' say what was so urgent, but wanted to meet for lunch; a small Vietnamese noodle shop up the street from the Tribune building.

Gil stuck his big head through my open door. He was a good guy and a good union man who came out of the trades; a souse chief for 20 years and a long time member of the E-Board of the local. When I resigned Gil had stepped into the President's spot. He had a head for finances and politics, something I sorely lacked. In exchange, I was given the senior BA at large position —made up especially for me—so I did pretty much what I wanted. Right now I wanted to take a leave of absence.

"Hell yes," Gil said. "With pay. And hold onto the car. Hell, this Local owes you."

"Thanks"

"That must have been pretty tough, that shit at the Hyatt. Too bad, Peter was a good union member."

"He was a nice man," I added, as Gil closed my door.

I opened the *L.A. Times* to the article on the Chinese immigrants, just as Gil opened the door again.

"I'll see to it his family gets the thousand dollar death benefit. It ain't much, but it's better than nothing."

"Thanks," I said and returned to the article.

> **LOS ANGELES**- Port workers and Immigrations officers made a grisly discover yesterday when they opened a freight container and discovered the bodies of twenty Chinese men and women. They had apparently died from lack of water and the heat in the locked container.

Immigration officer Mark Udall said the bodies were most likely those of illegal immigrants who had been abandoned by their smugglers for some unknown reason.

"We are discovering more and more of this sort of thing," Udall told the Times. "For some reason these unscrupulous smugglers must have feared the authorities and been tipped off and left these poor people to die."

The article went on, but I had read enough.

Before meeting Ted, I headed down to the Oaks Card Club where Johnny Wong tended bar during the day. I sat down at the bar and he poured me a double Jack Daniels as was our custom.

"Thanks." I took out a Lucky and Johnny was right there with a lighter.

"So, did you see Peter's niece? "he asked.

"Yeah,"

"And did you give her the pork bows?"

"Yeah. She asked how I knew it was customary to bring some kind of food when visiting. I told her it was a Jewish custom."

Johnny laughed.

I took out the slip of paper I had taken and handed it to him.

"What's this?" he asked.

"Found it on the stuffed panda bear the Chinese Consul had brought her. What do you make of it and why a panda?"

Johnny opened the note and studied it for a moment. I sipped my whiskey. It tasted good, warming my stomach and sending a sense of relaxation throughout my body, and I wondered why I had every gone on the wagon.

"Hmmm, our Peter Wu apparently was more than he seemed."

"What's it say?"

"Well, it's not a direct translation. But in essence it says: 'On behalf of the Chinese people we honor Major Ching–Shu Wu for his service to The People's Republic of China and offer our condolences to his niece May-lingWu who we are confident will take up the noble banner of her honorable uncle and continue in his work in the service of the government of the Peoples Republic.' What the fuck do you think this means, Smitty?"

"That's what I thought you could tell me."

"Shit if I know. Man, I told you Chinese shit is complicated and weird. But I'd guess it means Peter was into some shit I didn't know about. In fact, I don't think anyone did. Mei-ling's a nice lady, but I'd stay clear of her if I was you. This sounds like Chinese business."

I pulled out five bucks for the drink, and as part of our ritual, Johnny refused it.

"No brother. You're our union guy. You don't pay."

And also as part of the ritual I dropped it on the bar as a tip.

"I gulped down the rest of the Jack. "Johnny, he asked me to take care of her. I can't just ignore that."

Johnny shook his head as he transferred the fiver to his pants pocket. "Well, don't say I didn't warn you, brother."

* * *

# CHAPTER
# 6

I drove back to downtown Oakland and found a parking place two blocks from the restaurant. It was a hole in the wall called The Noodle Shop. It was supposes to have the best Vietnamese noodles this side of Saigon, or Ho Chi Minh City as the Communists renamed it after chasing us out. Ted swore they were as good as he had when he was there. All the ingredients were fresh and the noodles were home-made he said.

Ted had a thing about everything Asian, especially Vietnamese since coming back from covering the war. He finally completed his infatuation with Asia by marrying a beautiful Vietnamese woman. She was a doctor, trained in France at the Sorbonne, and she spoke English with a French accent. Ted's dream woman.

He was already there when I went in, sitting at a table reading the *San Francisco Chronicle*. He looked up as I sat down. "Well, at least they haven't got the story yet."

I sat down and picked up the menu, but Ted waved me off.

"I already ordered for both of us."

"Thanks, but maybe I'd like to make my own choice."

"You don't know what's good. Trust me."

"An older Vietnamese woman brought us two steaming bowls, set them down, and then scurried off as if we were GIs come to burn down her village; bad memories of war.

"You'll like this. It's not on the menu."

I looked at it. It smelled good, but I didn't recognize most of the things that were floating around.

"I always wondered what those menus on the wall said. What's in it?" I asked searching through the clear broth for something familiar.

"Don't ask, just eat."

We didn't talk as we slurped down the noodles and the spicy soup. He was right; it was strange, but good, especially the small pieces of soft chewy meat that were in abundance.

I finally wiped my face with the paper napkin. "So what's so important? Surely you didn't bring me here just to eat these noodles."

"They were good, weren't they?" he said authoritatively.

"You said it was urgent."

"It concerns your old bartender buddy and his niece."

"Yeah, I wanted to thank you for holding back the story. I didn't think you would."

"I didn't," he said looking down into his nearly empty bowl. "I wrote it all right; couldn't take a chance of the *Chronicle* scooping me."

"So?"

"That's why I called you. Have you gone and seen the niece, what's her name?"

"Mei-ling?"

"Yes, that's it. Mei-ling Wu. Or at least that's been her name since she came to the States in '71."

"So, what of it," I said. I think I sounded defensive, but it went over Ted's head.

"Anyway, I submitted my story. It was a damn good piece if I say so myself. Then, I get called into my editor's office. He tells me he's shit canning the story; that I should rewrite it from a local angle. No mention of Wu's past or his connection to the Red Army or the government of the PRC. That's People's Republic of China."

"Yeah Ted, I know what PRC is. So, what's it all mean?"

"It means he must have checked on the story and someone told him not to run it. Shit Smitty, this thing must be hot, and I'm being told to forget it."

"Who could dictate to the *Tribune*? What happened to freedom of the press and all that good shit?"

"My guess is he checked out my source, and that someone in the State Department put the kibosh on it."

"How can they do that?"

"National Security...had to be, and coming from someone pretty high up. My editor's a pretty square guy and a principled journalist, but with the changes going on at the paper, I guess he didn't want to ruffle no one's feathers. This thing could be dangerous and I don't want you ending up with your throat slit in some Chinatown alley like you almost did three years ago. I called to warn you off this woman."

"But what do you think's going on?" I said, growing really worried for Mei-ling. True I had just met the woman, but I was attracted to her and looking forward to seeing her that night. I didn't want anything to interfere in that. I decided to confide in Ted and told him about the note on the stuffed Panda.

"You're shitting me...the fucking Chinese Consulate?"

"Yeah, it even surprised my buddy who knows everything that goes on in Chinatown."

"So, our Captain was still connected with the Chinese government."

"Major. He was a Major according to the note on the stuffed panda," I said, smiling. It wasn't often I one upped Ted.

"Hmmmm. Guess he got a promotion since coming to the

States. All the more reason to keep clear of this woman. If they want her to fill in for the old bartender, she's got to be connected too."

"You think she's a spy?"

"Either that, or..."

"Or what?" I said.

"Or the Chinese are working on something with the State Department. Who knows? This kind of shit gets really mixed up."

"You mean our government would cooperate with the Communists, even after Tian'anmen?

"Hey, what are a few hundred Chinese dead students if something is in our self interest? Or, maybe he was a spy and they were monitoring him. Who knows? All we know is someone wanted to shut him up so bad they gunned him down in broad day light in public, and now the Chinese want your Ms. Wu to take his place."

"If you're right, why would they make such a public display of their relationship by going to pay their respects to Mei-ling and drawing attention to it?"

"Who knows? Maybe they're trying to flush out the bad guys and they're using her as bait. I told you this Chinese shit can get complicated. Steer clear of this."

""I don't think I can," I said. "I made a promise to a dying man, and when you make a promise like that you ought to keep it."

Ted laughed. "You know, that sounds like a line from The Maltese Falcon."

`"Yeah, me and Humphrey fucking Bogart."

Ted stood up. You get the tab, I gotta run." He stopped at the door. "By the way, that was offal in the noodles." And he disappeared into the street.

He left me staring at my empty bowl, a stomach full of innards and the unpaid tab.

* * *

# CHAPTER 7

They say Chinese are bad drivers because they're always looking for a parking place. Well, anyone who has looked for a place to park in Chinatown can well understand it. I drove past the house on Webster Street and the curbs were packed tighter than a can of Portuguese sardines. But apparently the rule didn't apply to the Ray-Ban guy sitting at the wheel of his Toyota sports car and parked directly across the street from Mei-ling's.

I turned down Seventh and circled the block; wall to wall cars. On my third pass I hit pay dirt; a spot, like a missing tooth exactly where the Toyota had been, as if Ray-Ban guy had purposefully left it for me. I didn't hesitate. As I backed into the spot an old Chinese guy came up right behind me in a VW bug and blasted his horn. We had a short Mexican standoff right there in the middle of Chinatown. He finally backed down and went around me shaking his fist. I could see his angry face glaring at me, as if to say "how dare this round eyed devil take my parking place. This is my territory". I just figured it was an important lesson in sharing.

The door opened and for a moment I lost by breath; Mei-ling standing there, her black shiny hair hanging down over a green silk cheongsam dress with an embroidered dragon twisting up her slim body until its head slithered up to her small breasts which appeared to be supported by the dragon's claws. The front of the dress was open just enough to show her cleavage and chest that was ornamented by a simple jade necklace. The slits in the dress came to her upper thighs. The dress itself reflected her emerald green eyes and her full lips were even more inviting than I remembered. If her intension was to turn me on she had succeeded. If not, I didn't care because the effect was the same as the blood rushed from my head to my groin.

"I'm so glad you could come, Smitty."

"You look lovely," I said clumsily.

She took my hand and led me to the parlor like we were old pals.

"Sit down and I'll fix us drinks. Vodka Martini?"

"Fine," I said, not wanting to tell her I preferred Bourbon. It was a good thing because she had apparently prepared the drinks ahead of time. She brought over two glasses and sat down next to me on the love seat. She put her free hand on my thigh in an unsuspected, but welcome, familiar gesture.

"So Smitty, tell me what it's like representing workers in a capitalist country."

I was surprised. It was a direct question. It sounded like something my committed socialist mother would have said. I took a gulp of the martini and could feel my face flush.

"Well, I can tell you it's frustrating. The cards are stacked against the employee and only the union stands between them and the boss. Your uncle told me in China the workers and the management worked together on an equal basis. Is that true?" I asked, turning the conversation back on her.

She smiled and looked in my eyes. "For the most part, yes. The union representative and the management are all members of the Communist Party, you see? If a manager is abusive the union can have him fired. Management and workers must be in harmony to create a productive environment. From what I see in America this is not true."

"But tell me," I said. "What's your story Mei-ling...?"

"My story?" she smiled, giving my thigh a little squeeze.

I started getting a hard on. It had been a long time since I had been this close to an attractive woman.

"If you mean how I came to America, there's nothing to tell," she smiled. "I came here several years before my Uncle joined me. I went to Berkeley on a scholarship from China. Since then I have been a student and now I lecture in Chinese history. I was surprised when I came here how little people know about China. After all, we are one of the largest countries in the world, and our economy will soon rival that of Japan, and maybe even America."

"But don't you have a boyfriend. Surely a beautiful woman like you has her pick of men."

She laughed and then kissed me on the cheek.

"You're sweet, Smitty."

It was obvious that it was none of my business.

At this she stood up. "I think it is time we eat..."

It was at that moment I saw a flash from outside the window, followed by a faint crack, like a firecracker. Without thinking I leaped from the love seat and tackled Mei-ling just as the front window exploded. The bullet hit the wall with a dull thud. A second bullet whizzed over our heads and crashed into one of the glass frames on the wall.

We both lay there not saying a word for what seemed like a long time. Slowly I became aware that I had fallen directly on top of her. Her dress was hiked up above her thighs and her legs were parted as my body rested between them. She was clinging tightly to me. Her fingernails, like the claws of a tiger, were digging into my back as if to prevent me from moving away. Her body was hot and throbbing against me. Then, as if it were a natural reaction, she began to slowly move her hips, pressing against me, emitting a low animal moan, and her breathing grew heavier. Suddenly I was transported to the back seat of my car in the drive-in movie, dry banging my high school girlfriend. They say that violence can excite the sexual drive, but at that moment I wasn't thinking about the psychology of fear. Just a moment ago she had nearly been killed, and now she was grinding a man who only two days before had been a complete stranger. I felt myself quickly reaching an orgasm. I came in a burst and my moan matched hers like an operatic love duet, and then I collapsed on top of her. We lay there for a few minutes, not saying a word and then I rolled off and lay next to her. She reached down and took my hand. We didn't look at one another or speak for awhile.

"Don't you think we should call the cops?" I finally managed to say.

"No," she said. "They'll just send Sergeant Fong. The man's on the take from every gangster in Chinatown."

"Can't you ask for someone else?"

"This is his beat," she said. "I think he's the only officer in the department who speaks Chinese. He's worthless."

I stood up on the hope that whoever it was that shot in the window had gone. Since I didn't get a bullet in the head I figured it was all clear. I offered my hand to Mei-ling and helped her up. It was as if nothing had happened between us, or we both refused to acknowledge it. Her face was flush. She was as embarrassed and surprised as I was by what had just happened.

"We have to get you out of here," I said.

I expected her to protest, but instead she said, "Where will I go?" She pulled her dress down and instinctively wiggled to make it fall straight.

I thought for a moment. The apartment on Lakeshore was out of the question.

"My boat," I said. "I have a boat in the Emeryville Marina. You'll be safe there."

She nodded and then smiled. "I'll get you a wash cloth to clean up."

I looked down. There was a wet spot on the front of my pants. "I'm sorry," I said. "It's been a long time since I've been with a woman."

"Its okay, Smitty. Some of that might be from me."

She headed for the door.

"You'd better pack a few things," I called after her.

She stopped and looked back at me. "Do you really think someone wants to kill me?"

"I'd say it's a good bet."

* * *

# CHAPTER 8

We didn't speak as I drove through Oakland toward Emeryville. I don't know if we were both in shock from the gun shot, or whether it was the unexpected act of adolescent passion. Maybe both.

I got onto San Pablo Avenue, the long stretch of road that starts in downtown Oakland and runs straight along the western border of the East Bay through Emeryville, Berkeley, El Cerrito and Richmond, all the way to where the Benicia Bridge crosses the Sacramento River.

I turned left off San Pablo onto Stanford and into Emeryville. Once a thriving industrial area, the small town was quickly becoming a sprawling urban shopping center as the city fathers past out development permits and tax incentives for unreported kickbacks. It was how things were done. Condos were displacing the small working class houses, and the large Black population was slowly being pushed into West Oakland.

The Marina is at the end of a long man-made stretch of land with office buildings, a Watergate apartment complex and several restaurants, as well as the Emeryville Fire Department. It was dark and there were only a few cars in public parking lot. A long strip of greenery ran along the Bay, separating it from the Emeryville Marina.

I used my key and opened the gate to the docks where hundreds of large and small boats were docked side by side. It was like a watery New York tenement; a place where people kept their pleasure craft, and where a lot of people called home. Most of the live-a-boards were friendly and minded their own business. No one would think of looking for a Chinese woman here. It was a perfect hideout, or so I told myself.

I led Mei-ling down the dimly lit dock to the end where my 42 foot Rough Water motor launch was birthed.

"Well, this is it," I said, and helped her on board.

Once in the cabin Mei-ling fell into the plush built-in couch and put her head back. Her eyes closed. Her long black hair flowed over her breast. The slit on her dress flopped open, revealing the golden slim legs that just an hour before had clung to me. I wanted to explore that exotic body and make proper love to her.

"I would like a drink. I spilled my last one," she said without moving. "Can you make a martini?"

"You must be hungry too," I said.

"No, just a drink."

"Well, I have some vodka, no ice. No vermouth or olives either. Don't get many calls for Martinis"

"Straight vodka will be fine," she sighed.

As I poured a glass of Stoli and some JD, both straight, she said, "Isaac, that's what your name is, yes?"

"Yes," I handed her the vodka. She took the drink.

"I think I will call you that. I like that better than Smitty. Is that okay?"

"The last woman who insisted on calling me Isaac I fell in love with," I said casually.

It had been in the year of the Loma Prieta earthquake. The slim lawyer and I had been through a lot together defending a bartender at the Golden Gate Fields race track who was being framed for robbery and murder. But, when it was done, she was done, and I was left out in the cold. No matter.

"Okay, that's what I'll call you."

"It sounds good when you say it. Maybe I'll fall in love with you," I half joked.

She looked down at her drink. Her hand was shaking and she had to steady it with the other. "Delayed reaction," she laughed uneasily. "I'm very tired, Isaac. Where will I sleep?"

"The aft cabin. There's a double bed, a shower and head... bathroom."

"I know what a head is," she said as she stood up.

"Look, about what happened earlier, I..."

She put her fingers over my mouth. "Hush. It's okay. I was quite scared and you distracted me from my fear. It's been a long time since I felt the weight of a man on top of me. And you were on top of me, Isaac."

"Yes, I'm sorry about that."

"It's all right. It was quite pleasurable."

"I was trying to protect..."

"Never mind. Just show me the cabin and we will talk in the morning."

I took her down the two steps that opened into the master's stateroom. It had a double bed with book shelves along the side, and two oval port windows that were covered by curtains.

"Quite homey," she said.

I quickly showed her how to work the head and the shower, and then she led me to the cabin door.

"Now, I must get some sleep." She kissed me gentle on my lips. "Thank you, Isaac Thank you for everything."

And I was back in the salon alone. I sat at the dinette, poured another JD, and lit up a Lucky. Two days ago I was just a run of the mill frustrated business agent and now I was falling in love and up to my neck in Chinatown intrigue and murder. "Christ Smitty, what the fuck are you doing?"

* * *

# CHAPTER 9

It was still dark outside when I woke up with a slight headache and a crick in my neck. It was past twelve when I had finally dropped off to sleep in one of the forward staterooms that were crowded with storage. I threw on a clean pair of pants, got the coffee started and went out quietly so as not to wake Mei-ling.

The dark sky was turning gray and there was a chill in the air. I walked down the quiet dock to the gate and out to the parking lot. There were already several fishermen staring at their poles and sipping from steaming cups. I drove down to the Market that serviced the Watergate Apartment complex. They had just opened and I got a couple of bagels, cream cheese, lox, and some groceries to stock the boat, and then drove back to the docks.

I was surprised to see Mei-ling sitting at the dinette with a cup of coffee. She was wearing my white terry cloth robe that hung partially open in the front exposing just enough smooth flesh as to entice me to want more. She looked up as I stepped into the salon.

"Hi. Where have you been?"

"Got us some breakfast. Hope you like bagels and cream cheese."

"Love them. I took a shower and borrowed your robe, but I couldn't find the belt. I hope you don't mind?" she said, standing up and facing me. "About last night," she said with a strange smile on her face, and then she placed her hands on my chest and let the robe open. "I was very tired, but this morning I am awake," and she rose onto her tip toes and kissed me. Her lips widened invitingly as she pressed her naked body against me. I was not about to resist. It was like a dream. She slowly unbuttoned my flannel shirt...


We lay naked side by side in the double bed. I admired her slender shapely body and small breasts, firm with large brown nipples that had seemed to have a life of their own when I ran my lips over them. There had been no prerequisite oral preliminaries that every woman I had ever been with over the past twenty years demanded. Even Jasmine's love making now seemed somehow mechanical compared to Mei-ling's abandoned passion. For over an hour I was in what seemed a drug induced state of ecstasy.

The sun broke through the morning overcast and filtered in through the port window, casting a golden light into the stateroom. Mei's black hair was bunched up over the top of her head so she looked like a smooth bronze statue. We had both satiated our loneliness and hunger. Perhaps this was how she expressed her pain at the death of her uncle. The thought brought me reluctantly back to reality.

"Mei."

She looked over at me, and I almost drifted back into nirvana by her smiling dreamy emerald eyes. But there were some questions I needed answered and I ploughed ahead.

"Mei. It's none of my business, but I was wondering why

48

you haven't shown any emotion over your uncle's death?" I asked, feeling immediately like a shmuck.

Any other woman – any western woman – would have turned to ice, but Mei-ling was generous. She smiled, and I could see the sadness in her eyes.

"Isaac. In my culture we are brought up to not express our emotions in public. We are Buddhist. We believe that death is just an extension of our existence; that our life is just part of our passage. Now he is with our ancestors."

I know I was out of line, but my curiosity had to be satisfied. I had to know as much as I could about this woman that had come into my life. My pledge to the old bartender had now become personal. There were things I needed to know so I could do what I had to do to protect her.

"But, how could your uncle have been Buddhist when he was a communist? Aren't communists supposed to be atheists?" I asked.

"It's a long story. Are you sure you want to hear it?"

I nodded lamely.

"My mother and my uncle were raised Buddhist. They lived in a village in Guangdong Province in the south where they both joined the Communist Youth organization when they were young. Chinese peasants were treated very badly in feudal China, and the Nationalists, who controlled the government after the death of Sun Yet-sen, were not much better."

"Sun Yet-sen? I heard that name."

"He is like what your George Washington is to you Americans," she explained. "Anyway my father had been an organizer for the Communists and it was logical that we would join. Then, my father was murdered by the Nationalists and they declared war on the Communists."

She went on to explain how her uncle and mother had to join what she called the Long March north along with the rest of the Communist Army after General Chiang Kai-Shek and his

Nationalist Army defeated them in battle. She leaned over me. I could feel the erect dark nipples brush across my own hairless chest, and her long silky black hair draped over me.

"I don't want to bore you, Isaac. Those were confusing times with many competing forces, all vying for control of China."

"No, no. I want to know everything about you," I said.

She gently kissed me. I wasn't sure why she was attracted to me, but I didn't care. It had been three years since I had felt like this with a woman. The last time didn't last long and turned out badly. This time I hoped would be different.

She leaned on her elbow and continued. She said her uncle and mother survived the Long March while tens of thousands were killed.

"My uncle was only fourteen and my mother just eleven. Luckily they had been assigned to a small unit led by a brilliant young officer. They were very resourceful and managed to make it to the north. There, under the leadership of the Great leader, the Communist Army regrouped and fought their way back south.

"The civil war went on until the Japanese invaders came," she went on in a matter-of-fact way, as if she were giving a lecture to a room full of ignorant Occidentals, and I guess she was, because while my parents had made sure I knew all about the Russian revolution, I had no idea about the Chinese.

"The Communists and the Nationalist joined forces in a shaky United Front against the invaders until the war ended and the Japanese surrendered to the allies," she continued. "The fact is, the Communist proved brave fighters against the enemy, while the Nationalists held back, allowing the Americans and British to do most of the fighting for them so they would be strong enough to take up where they had left off; killing Communists. The future of China was at stake. Chaing ruled like a military dictator. His government was corrupt and brutal. Millions of Chinese peasants and workers joined the Communist struggle.

I was born just after the victory over Chaing who was forced to retreat to Taiwan in 1949 with what remained of his army and government. By then my Uncle Peter had become a highly respected ranking officer in the People's Liberation Army, and was on the Central Military Commission. He was put in charge of intelligence against counter-revolution in our home province. My mother died giving birth to me in 1951. My uncle made sure I was well cared for by our family when he was sent to Korea, and later he took care of me as if I was his own daughter. Anyway, that's modern Chinese history 1A, Isaac."

I had been listening, but not listening. My eyes were glued to her naked torso and I felt myself getting aroused again; a surprise since I hadn't been able to do that in many years, that is, get a hard-on so soon after having sex. She also noticed the bulge in the sheets and eased her hand down and held me.

"You're the first person I know who got so turned on by the Chinese Revolution," she smiled, and before I knew her lips where engulfing me. I ran my fingers over her smooth legs and she spread them invitingly. My tongue was soon searching out her most sensitive parts. It was quiet except for our mutual moans of ecstasy which soon built to a shared climax. I knew then that I would never tire of making love to this woman. It was a feeling I had never had with any woman, and I had known my share

"Well Isaac, now I would like to have a bagel," she finally said.

I watched as she slipped out of the bed, admiring her perfectly sculptured back as she wrapped the robe around her. She peeked over her shoulder as I stupidly gawked at her.

"Well, Isaac, are you going to fix me a bagel and cream cheese, and, what did you call it, lox?" and she disappeared up the steps into the salon.

I slipped into my pants and hurried after her like a puppy dog.

"This is good," Isaac. "But your lox is just smoked salmon?"

"You have cream cheese on your nose," I laughed as I poured the steaming coffee. "It's Jewish smoked salmon."

She giggled like a girl and wiped the white smudge onto a napkin. "What makes it Jewish. Does it dislike Palestinians?"

I laughed. "No silly girl. It's more an Eastern European thing. I think it has something to do with how it's smoked. Its Kosher," I said sitting across from her at the dinette. "So, you haven't told me how you and your uncle ended up here in Oakland."

"Well Isaac, like I said, my Uncle was pretty high up in the party. I was a student at the University in Guangzhou. I was studying Chinese history and had become a teacher. My professors all supported the Revolution and many were veterans of the war. They were Marxists, not fanatical Maoists, which was growing very popular with many students at the time. They believed the revolution would free them to teach."

"Bad move," I said, drawing on my limited knowledge of the Cultural Revolution.

"Very good, Isaac. Things were changing in China. There was a power struggle in the leadership. My Uncle found out that Mao was preparing an assault on what were being called bourgeois elements in society. It was really a power play against his perceived enemies in the Party. . . Isaac, this is really good coffee."

"It's Peets. You must have heard of it, you going to UC. You never had Peets?

"No, I really like it. Peets. I'll remember that."

"Yeah, but they'll probably franchise it and it will lose its uniqueness. Pretty soon gourmet coffees will be all over the place."

"Yes, capitalism works that way, doesn't it?" She laughed. "Anyway, Uncle Peter got wind of things to come. Student groups were already demonstrating at the University. He figured they wouldn't touch the Army, but he was worried about me. He pulled some strings and I got a scholarship to UC Berkeley through a University in Hong Kong. He arranged for me to go to the United States. And so here I am."

"And I'm glad you are," I said. "But what about your Uncle?"

"Well, Isaac. Several years into the Cultural Revolution the purges started reaching into the Army. Uncle Peter knew he was suspect of not being "revolutionary" enough because he had spoken out against the purges. His more cautious comrades in the military urged him to leave, and arranged for his escape to San Francisco where he claimed political asylum. I hope that answers your question, Isaac," she said. She took a bite of the bagel. "I like this lox."

My eyes kept drifting to the open robe, and despite having seen everything she had to offer, I still wanted to catch a peek of her perfect breasts, maybe an exposed nipple. It excited me. I wanted to drag her back into the aft cabin or make love to her right there in the salon. But there were still things I wanted to know.

I kept at her. "So your uncle was granted asylum. How's he end up at the Oakland Hyatt?"

"Like all immigrants, Isaac, Uncle Peter was sent to learn a vocation after going through what they call debriefing. He moved in with me in my small apartment near Chinatown, and went to bartending school. When the Hyatt opened up he was hired as a bar helper as part of the affirmative action agreement made with the city. The rest you know."

She ate the last bite of the bagel and again got cream cheese on her nose, only this time I leaned over and licked it clean. She took a napkin and wiped her face, as if in rejection of my affection. I could tell she was getting tired of answering my questions, but a persisted anyway.

"None of this explains why someone shot your uncle in cold blood and then tried to kill you," I said.

Her face changed. I was treading where I shouldn't and I knew it.

"That's all, Isaac. I want to get dressed now."

She got up and disappeared down the steps into the master stateroom. I hoped I hadn't blown it with her.

\* \* \*

# CHAPTER 10

I headed for the Oaks Club on San Pablo. I told Mei I was going to pick up her clothes and anything else she needed from the house. She wanted to come, but I insisted she stay put on the boat. I wanted to talk to Johnny and see if he had heard anything new on why Peter was killed.

It was nearly eleven when I sat down at the bar. The card room was already abuzz with players trying to earn back what they had lost the night before, or fleecing the suckers for every nickel. Johnny poured me a glass of Jack Daniels.

"How's it going, Smitty. Hear you've taken up with Peter's niece. Good looking little egg roll."

"How the hell you hear that?" I said.

"Man, don't nothing happen in Chinatown I don't hear about. You were seen leaving her place with her in tow. Word travels fast; especially when it's one of the community celebrities' niece and a white guy. And Peter was well known in Chinatown as you know."

"If that's right, Johnny, you must know why someone blew Peter away in the Hyatt basement."

He started wiping the bar with his towel, nervous like. "Some things that happen in Chinatown nobody knows, Smitty."

"Come on Johnny. You must know something."

He kept wiping the bar for a minute and then threw the towel over his shoulder. "Well, maybe something. I don't know if it means anything."

"Talk to me, brother."

"Well, at dinner last night my father mumbled; "This is no good, this Peter Wu thing." That's all he said. Just that, and then he went back to eating. Well, it was strange because my father never says anything at dinner. He just eats and listens as us kids jabber on about all kinds of bullshit stuff; never comments, never scolds, just listens and eats. If he has something important to say to us, it's never at dinner with my mother and auntie there."

"So...is that all he said?"

"Well, yes, at dinner anyway. After dinner he called me into his study where he smokes and does business. He said he was telling me what was going on because I am his Number One son and someday I would have to make decisions and represent the family and the Association. He said the Association was very concerned about the shooting. Even though it was at the Hyatt, it was giving Chinatown a bad name, and our plans for building the Cultural Center and revitalizing Chinatown could be jeopardized. He said that he had been contacted by the Mayor who was very concerned. Look Smitty, I been knowing you a long time and don't want nothing bad to happen to you. I told you to stay out of Chinatown shit..."

"It's too late, Johnny. I'm in it now."

He looked around, as if he expected someone was listening. "Smitty, you meet me after my shift is over. I'll be at Jack London Square, down by the Potomac dock. You know the place?"

I nodded; FDR's restored personal yacht was docked behind

the Port Commission's office building by the ferry dock.

"There's too many long ears in this place. Too many Chinese gamblers, and I'm not sure about those guys working in the kitchen. We can talk better there. You meet me."

"I'll be there," I said and started to get up from the bar.

"Hey Smitty. You didn't finish your drink."

I couldn't hurt his feelings. I gulped it down and handed him five bucks which he promptly refused as was our custom. I tried to lay it down for a tip but he shook his head. "You going to need all the dough you can get if you're going to get involved in Chinatown shit, Smitty."


Small miracles happen and I found a parking spot almost in front of Mei's house. I took out the key she had given me, but saw the door was ajar.

Someone had been there and didn't make a secret of it. Shit was everywhere – papers strewn all over the floor, furniture turned over – it was a mess. I didn't hear anything. Whoever had been there must have left, or so I thought. The front door shut with a bang and I swung around. I had been caught from behind once in my life and had ended up in the hospital for a week in a coma. I'd be damned if that was going to happen again. It was the Ray-Ban man.

"I've been waiting for you to show up, Mr. Smith. Or do they call you Smitty?"

I started to make a move but a small gun suddenly appeared in the man's hand, and I decided not to be a dead hero.

"So, you found me. You do this?" I said, nodding my head toward the upturned room.

"No, that's not my style. They must have come sometime in the night."

"Nice surveillance work," I said sarcastically, hoping his Chinese humor grasped the subtlety.

"Well, can't be everywhere all the time, Smitty. Man gotta relax some time." he smiled.

This was no FOB gangster. He slipped the gun back into the pocket of his jacket.

"So, I don't suppose you're going to tell me where Mei-ling Wu is," he said.

"I'd say you were right, that is, if I knew where Mei-ling Wu was."

Well, in any case, do me a small favor."

"Depends," I said.

He pulled a business card from his pocket and stuck it out for me to take. "Give her this; that is if you happen to run into her."

I reached over and took the card and glanced at it. It was in Chinese characters. I should have studied Chinese in school, but who knew?

"If I happen to run into her," I said, casually slipping the card into my shirt pocket.

"And friend," he added. "I'd bow out of this if I were you. This ain't no union grievance you can fix in arbitration. You could get seriously hurt."

"Thanks, I'll keep that in mind"

"You do that." He turned to go.

"Oh," I said. "Lose the Ray-Bans, pal They look stupid."

He turned around as he put the shades on. "Oh, I think they look rather cool." And he was out the door.

I found Mei-ling's room. Her clothes were strewn all over the floor and on the bed, but I gathered some things up I thought she could use. I was particularly choosy with her lingerie, and she had some pretty sexy things. I wasn't her first boy friend. I threw it all into a paper bag. Johnny didn't get off until two so I decided to head for the Ringside and grab a pastrami sandwich.

The Ringside was a tiny bar down from the Tribune Tower on

13th Street. Both were historical landmarks, but the Ringside wasn't listed. It should have been. It was where all the *Tribune* reporters once drank. But those days were gone, and the owner, an ex-fighter named Eddy, kept threatening to sell out. I tried to convince him not to. The Ringside was my office away from the office. Besides, Eddy served Guinness on tap and I could get excellent pastrami on fresh rye from the Jewish deli down the street that was run by Chinese.

"The usual," Eddy said as I sat at the long bar. There were pictures of fighters all along the back wall which you could almost touch by reaching behind you. Most of them were signed. The fighters had all fought at the old arena in the Kaiser Center when fighting was big in Oakland.

"Sure, and order me a ..."

"Yeah, yeah. Pastrami on rye. Got you covered Smitty."

Eddy went back to handling the new patrons coming in on their lunch break. I was glad to see him doing some business.

Eddy had been a top light weight contender. Now all he had to show for years of boxing was a scarred up face, huge arthritic knuckles and the Ringside. I'd hate to see him give it up.

I went to the rear of the bar where there was a pay phone and called the union hall. Marta's harsh voice answered:

"Union Hall."

"Marta," I said. "It's Smitty."

"Smitty. I thought you were on leave?" There was an accusatory tone in her voice.

"Yeah, but I thought someone might have called the hall for me."

"Your buddy from the *Tribune* called a couple of times. And Smitty, there was an FBI guy came around asking for you."

"FBI?"

"Damn it Smitty, you people told me this place had cleaned up and was a safe place to work," she exploded. "I got three kids and I need to be around for them. I can't be involved with nothin' illegal. I'll sue you and the god damn union..."

"Okay okay," I said. "Calm down. There's nothing going on. It was probably just in connection with the murder..."

"Well, it better be. I'll report this whole damn place to the cops..."

I hung up. Marta's naked anger and threats were the last thing I needed. She should call her union if she got complaints. I missed Lily.

I tried Ted at his office but they said he was out, so I just returned to the bar and tried to enjoy my pastrami on rye and Guinness until it was nearly time to meet Johnny.


"Smuggling?" I said, not believing what Johnny had just said. "I don't believe it."

He was smoking cigarette after cigarette, looking around as if someone was hiding near us on the long empty dock.

"Well, not for sure, but my father's brother's cousin who works at a Russian restaurant on Clement Street in San Francisco said he saw Peter there having tea with a couple of known Chinese gangsters. Triad guys, he said. You know who they are, Smitty?"

"Some kind of Chinese gang?"

"Bigger and more ruthless than your Italian mafia, Smitty. Anyway, a couple of the Triads are now active Stateside since the crackdown in Hong Kong; drugs and illegal immigrants and god knows what else. Anyway, our Peter Wu was meeting with them, and my old man says it could be very bad for Oakland Chinatown."

"I don't get it," I said. "How could one meeting with some alleged gangsters cause your father problems?"

He glanced around and lit up another cigarette from the one he had just puffed down to a filter. You don't understand, Smitty. You saw how respected Peter was. When he came over here he was honored as a hero of the War of Liberation. No one in Chinatown particularly liked the Cultural Revolution and they welcomed Peter into the fold. He was made a member of many Chinese organizations. My father's association made him an honorary member a few years ago. But now, with the shooting, if the cops connect Peter with the triads, well it will be bad for everyone, Smitty."

"It don't make sense," I said.

"Sure it does. Peter was an officer in the Red Army."

"Yeah?"

"Well, think about it, Smitty. Peter was head of intelligence and security in Guangdong province. That's where most of the illegal immigrants and drugs come from. It's a very poor part of China. A lot of the older families in Chinatown came from Guangdong. With Peter's connections back home he would be a natural in helping smooth the way for smugglers."

"Well, maybe," I said. "But it's hard for me to believe Peter would do something like that. He wasn't the type."

"To tell the truth, Smitty, I don't believe it either, and I told my father that. But he didn't buy it. My father is a very suspicious man; hates the commies, especially Mao; old school Chinese. Anyhow, that's it. Now I have to go. Promised the old man I'd work at the market."

"Just one more thing, Johnny. Can you translate this card for me?" I handed him the business card the Ray-Ban man gave me.

He gave it a quick glance. "Shit Smitty, where'd you get this?"

"What's it say?"

He put his hand on my shoulder. "It says you better bail out before you end up dead. I can't help you no more, brother." He threw his cigarette down and walked away.

\* \* \*

# CHAPTER 11

I wondered around Jack London Square, my mind racing. How was it possible that Peter Wu, the quiet unassuming Chinese bartender, was tied into illegal smuggling and Chinese gangsters? It just didn't jive. But then again, who would have expected him to be a Chinese Communist hero and a Major in the Red Army.

I found myself sitting under the brass statue of Jack London. Jack London, the socialist, world reknown author, union organizer and defender of working people. I had idolized him until I discovered that he meant all working people except the Chinese. Jack London, the famous writer of such classics as "Call of the Wild" and "White Fang" also wrote "The Yellow Peril" and some other book—I couldn't remember the title— warning that the Chinese would take over, not just America but the entire world, if nothing else, just by their sheer numbers. As I recalled he had actually called for the genocide of the Chinese race. How ironic, me, a union rep, organizer and socialist, now in the midst of Chinese intrigue, protecting a Chinese woman who I was falling for, after defending her uncle, the ex-Chinese Red Army officer who was also a member of my union ... the very people London so feared. It made my head swim.

I shook it off, needing a drink to clear my head from London's poison hatred and racism, so I headed to The Grotto, the only Union restaurant left in the Square, and had a double JD while forcing myself back to reality. I wasn't sure exactly what that was anymore, and worse, didn't really care.

It was near five when I drove down Sanford toward the marina. My heart pounded in expectation of seeing Mei-ling. I felt a little foolish, like some school kid with a crush.

I decided to stop and pick up something for Mei at the Hong Kong East Ocean Restaurant that sat like an emperor's palace over-looking the Bay from the Marina. I had left Mei hours ago. Surely she would appreciate something to eat and maybe it would soften her up enough to answer some questions. Besides, the restaurant had some of the best Chinese food around; pricey but good. Of course, it wasn't union ... it was Chinese.

I walked past the hostess to the cashier's desk to order take-out when I spotted her. She was sitting at a window table with a martini in front of her and wearing the same sexy green dress she had worn the night before. Her hair was up in a tidy bun with a tortoise shell and pearl comb. Her legs were crossed exposing a lovely golden thigh.

"Can I help you?" the cashier said.

"No, I'm joining a friend," I said, and walked into the restaurant.

She must have seen my reflection in the window.

"Isaac. How did you know I was here?"

She was so beautiful I was at a loss for words. All the shit that had piled up in my brain vanished.

"I ... I didn't. I was stopping to pick you up some food." I stammered.

"I'm glad you did. We can eat together," she said smiling, as if she hadn't nearly been killed by an assassin's bullet the evening before. It was as if we were on a casual dinner date.

I sat down and ordered a double JD from a passing waiter. I could feel myself getting pissed off again. Her cavalier attitude bugged the shit out of me. "What the hell are you doing here? I told you to stay on the boat."

"Calm down. Nobody would think to look for me here, Isaac. I was hungry and I didn't know when you'd be back. Besides, my uncle knew the owner, and we'd been here a couple of times to eat. In fact the owner, Mr. Po, saw me when I came in and offered his condolences. I could see he was genuinely concerned about my uncle. I told him he was on his way back to rest with our ancestors in Taishan where he was born. This seemed to make him happy. He told me to sit down. Dinner was on him. He would take care of everything. So, you see, it was good I came in."

"Goddamnit, Mei. I don't get you. Someone's trying to kill you and you don't seem to even care."

"Isaac dear, why would anyone want to kill me? It was just a mistake. Now let's enjoy dinner."

I reached over the table, nearly knocking over her martini, and grabbed her wrist.

"Damnit Mei, you're not telling me the truth. I've been told twice today to throw your ass to the wolves and take a hike or I'd end up like Peter. Now I want the truth!"

"Please Isaac..."

I suddenly realized that I was making a spectacle of myself, and people were looking at me as if I was some kind of Meshugeh. I figured I'd better cool it before I was dragged out of there in cuffs, or worse, a straight jacket.

"Okay, okay, I'm sorry, Mei. But I want the truth goddammit," I said, lowering my voice.

"Alright, my dear Isaac. Wait until after we eat and are back on the boat and I promise I'll tell you everything I can so you don't throw me to the lions."

"Wolves."

"Yes, wolves. I wouldn't like that. But now, let's enjoy our dinner. After all, it is our first date."

The waiter brought over my JD and set it down gingerly as if trying not to upset me again.

Dinner lasted over an hour as waiters kept bringing small dishes with different things; some fried, some baked, some jelled, and some steamed. So many tastes and textures I had a hard time deciding which ones I liked and which ones really repelled me, and I had no idea what it was I was eating. Mei explained to me that what we were having was not on the menu. It was called Dim Sum which was on the menu, but she explained that many of the dishes were special, and not served to the regular customers. I took that to mean white people. I had always wondered what those lists in Chinese on the walls of restaurants were. Now I knew: Chinese only.

I was just beginning to relax, sipping the last of my drink when a well dressed elderly man came up to our table. Mei -ling introduced me, but I could see he wasn't interested in her round eyed friend. He spoke to her in Chinese, and even though I didn't understand a word, I could hear the urgency in his voice.

Mei stood up. "Come Isaac, we must go."

"Huh?"

"Don't argue. Just come."

We followed the man, Mr. PO, out of the dining room and into the kitchen. He rushed us past the dozen cooks who were jabbering in Chinese. They ignored us, and then we were at the back door.

"You can slip out here," Po said in English.

The next thing I knew we were standing in front of a large dumpster that stunk of rotting fish. The sky was turning dark as night came on.

"What was all that about?" I asked Mei. She was pressing up against me.

"Mr. Po said two suspicious men were asking about me. He said he told the hostess to keep them busy the best she could, but he wasn't sure if they saw us leave."

"Shit, we'd better get back to the boat," I said, grabbing her hand and starting toward the dock which was a good ways from the restaurant.

"But what about your car?"

"That's the first place they'll look if they saw us," I said. "We better make our way back on foot."

"Okay Isaac. Whatever you say." And then she pulled a small automatic pistol from her purse and snapped a bullet into the chamber.

"What the fuck," I said.

"Don't worry Isaac; I know how to use it." And she allowed me to lead her.

We hurried along the path alongside the marina. Suddenly I heard the crack of a gunshot. I glanced back and saw two shadowy figures racing after us. Another flash and crack. I felt the bullet wiz past my head. Mia Ling pulled loose from me, and I stopped to see her kneel and fire her pistol. The men disappeared behind some trees.

"Let's go, Isaac," Mei said, grabbing my arm.

We ran blindly along the dirt path until we got to my dock. The sun was setting, and I hoped the long shadows would conceal us. I didn't relax until we were safely beyond the locked gate. I felt my heart pounding, and I was breathing hard as we hurried along the dark dock to the boat. I helped Mei on board and then followed her into the cabin where I was able to start the engine. The low growl of the large Perkins diesel was soothing.

"What are you doing, Isaac?"

"We can't stay here. They'll be searching for us. I don't know who those guys are, but they want you dead, and I ain't going to let that happen."

* * *

# CHAPTER 12

I sat her down at the dinette, went outside to untie us from the dock and disconnect the shore power. Back on board, I went up to the upper deck helm, switched on the running lights and eased out of the birth toward the opening of the marina and into the bay.

A rare warm evening breeze blew in off the San Joaquin Valley, as the boat sliced through the dark water. The lights of the Bay Bridge and the San Francisco skyline sparkled off the water as the Emeryville Marina faded behind us. The tension of the last hour melted away. I hadn't thought of where I would go, just that we had to get away from Emeryville, so I headed out onto the Bay.

Mei joined me on the upper deck. She had changed out of the Green dress and was wearing tight blue hip hugging jeans with a loose Cal Bears tee shirt. She came toward me. She was barefoot. Exotic perfection. She put her arms around my waist and pressed her small body softly against my back.

"It's so beautiful," she said in a near whisper.

It was a perfect romantic moment, until I burst out; "What the hell's going on, Mei?"

Her hands slipped away from me and she leaned against the instrument panel with her hands behind her.

"You're right Isaac; you deserve to know; only the night is so beautiful. Can't we talk about this later? Right now I just want to enjoy being here with you."

I looked at her. The rising moon cast a blue light that illuminated her face, and the wind whipped through her shiny black hair, making her even sexier. All of a sudden I didn't really care about anything but the sight of her.

"You are so beautiful. We don't need to talk now."

The silhouette of Angel Island grew closer. I had decided we would anchor off the leeward side of the island for the night while I decided where we would go. In the meantime, it would give us some time alone.

I slowed down. The shore of the island, sitting in the middle of the Bay, was illuminated in the blue light of the full moon.

"What are those buildings? Mei asked, pointing toward the institutional looking structures sitting along the shoreline.

"It's the old immigration station," I said. "It's where people coming into the U.S. where held, mostly Chinese; kinda like Ellis Island in New York. It hasn't been open for a long time"

"Yes, I have read about it," she said.

"We can go ashore in the morning if you're interested. We'll anchor here for the night."

"Without my asking, Mei hurried down to the deck, first going to the stern and letting out the line of my small dingy. She then made her way to the bow and motioned to me, indicating she stood ready to release the anchor. She obviously had experience on boats.

I motioned for her to let go the anchor, and like an experienced sailor she released the power wench and the anchor dropped into the still water, reeling out chain and rope. When it stopped, she motioned me again to back off too allow enough scope on the line. "

I reversed the engines and slowly backed off as Mei released the line, allowing the anchor to set securely.

"Okay," she shouted and waved her hand.

I cut the engine. The anchor held fast.

"Where the hell did you learn to handle boat lines like that?"

Mei laughed as she poured herself a glass of straight vodka.

"I was a year in the People's Maritime Militia. You want one?"

"Bourbon thanks."

"I was assigned to a boat very much like yours, only it had a fifty caliber machine gun mounted on the front."

She brought the drinks over to the dinette and sat across from me.

"Can I have one of your cigarettes?"

"Help yourself." I said, throwing my pack of Luckys on the table. She dumped one out and put it between her lips. I reached across and lit it for her, and then lit my own.

She belted down the vodka in one gulp, as if she were at a Russian wedding toasting the happy couple. This was a side of Mei I hadn't seen. She noticed me staring at her.

"We had a Russian advisor on board. He taught me how to drink vodka. He taught me many things."

"I don't want to hear it," I said.

"Anyway, we patrolled the coast down to Vietnam." She laughed. "Almost got into a shooting match with one of your American Coast Guard."

I took a long drag off my smoke, and followed it with a sip of whiskey.

"You're just full of surprises," I said.

"We had a hostile American army killing tens of thousands of Vietnamese comrades on our southern border. We didn't know if we would be next. We were defending our country."

"Yes, I remember. I managed to avoid the draft, and was involved in the peace movement," I said, trying to distance myself from the war.

"It's all right, Isaac. No one blamed the American people for the crimes of your government. But let's not talk about that."

She poured another shot of vodka, downed it and reached her hand out to me.

"Come Isaac, let's shower and climb into bed."

I didn't play hard to get....

\* \* \*

# Chapter 13

Mei-ling ran her hand lovingly over the Chinese characters that were carved into the crumbling cement wall of the large dormitory where thousands of Chinese languished for months on end, waiting to be allowed into the country or sent back to China. It was a dark period in American history when Chinese immigrants were barred from the country unless they could prove they already had family here.

The Immigration Station had been slowly decaying since its closure in 1940, three years before the Chinese Exclusion Act was repealed. I thought of Jack London and wondered how an intelligent man could have so much fear of fellow human beings because they didn't look like him—how an entire nation could summon up such hatred and paranoia.

I watched as Mei-ling seemed to be communicating with the past ghosts that had authored the elaborate characters in the wall.

"What do they say?" I asked in a feeble attempt to be part

of her experience.

"These were educated people - poets and scholars - they should never have suffered such indignities," she said, more to herself than me. I could see tears welling up in her eyes.

Before I could get to her in the hopes of putting my arm around her comfortingly, she abruptly turned around, angrily wiped the tears from her eyes and brushed past me on her way out.

"Come on, Isaac, this place depresses me."

We spent the rest of the day walking around Angel Island. It was another beautiful day, and it seemed hundreds of people had come to the island on the ferry from San Francisco. Children were running all over the place, screaming and carrying on the way kids do when set free in the open spaces. We grabbed a couple of hot dogs from the snack bar on the other side of the Island where the ferry came in as Mei's dark mood melted away and she caressed my arm.

We explored the interior of the Island, laying side by side in the sun, and just enjoying one another's company like a couple of young lovers.

It was getting dark by the time we got back to the spot where I had tied up the dinghy, and I rowed back out to the boat. We weighed anchor and headed for Sausalito for dinner at the Spinnaker.

The lights of San Francisco were coming on as the sky turned a dark purple. We had scored window seats with its panoramic view from the Richmond Bridge to the San Francisco skyline and the Golden Gate Bridge.

Mei took my hand. "Thank you Isaac. I enjoyed myself today."

I took her hand to my mouth and kissed it. *Shmaltzey*, yes, but I was in love.

The waiter came to the table and handed us menus while informing us of the day's specials. He wore a white shirt and tie, looking more like a young executive than a waiter. I guessed him to be a student working his way through college. I doubted the place was union. Few restaurants outside Oakland and San Francisco were, and those were getting rare. Nevertheless, I had to admire the young man's professionalism.

We sipped at our drinks, glancing over the menus until the waiter came back, asking if we had decided.

"What do you suggest?" I asked.

"The seafood is very good," he said. "Myself, I'm from Idaho and I prefer the New York steak."

After a good natured laugh Mei ordered Swordfish and I ordered the New York, rare.

"Good choices," our waiter smiled. "May I recommend a wine pairing?"

I ordered a house red and Mei another martini.

We didn't talk much through dinner. The food was exceptionally good and we were both hungry.

Mei stared out over the panoramic window at the night lights sparkling around the Bay. I looked at her, wondering how I had gotten so lucky.

"We have to go back," she said, avoiding eye contact..

"Why not just take off. My fuel tanks are full and we could head south..."

"That would be impossibly sweet Isaac. You know that," she answered turning her jade eyes on me.

"Yes, I know. I just hoped..."

"Will that be all," the waiter said, interrupting us.

"Another Martini," Mei said, smiling at the handsome fellow.

"A double Jack Daniels and the check,"

\* \* \*

# Chapter 14

After weighing anchor Mei had slipped below and changed into her shorts and T-shirt. She joined me on the upper deck where I was starting up the engine.

"We have to talk," Isaac. "I have to tell you everything I can, so you know what you've gotten into. I never meant for you to get caught up in this."

I leaned into her from the wheel and kissed her on the forehead, as I set a course for the Berkeley Marina. Emeryville was out of the question. The two Chinese thugs would be watching for us.

She pulled back. "No Isaac. This is not your problem."

For a moment I felt hurt and rejected, but I quickly dismissed it.

"Look, for whatever reason, your Uncle asked me to watch

over you. He asked in his dying breath, and now it's my job and I intend on seeing it through. Besides, I think I'm falling for you."

She lightly brushed her fingers across my cheek.

"That's sweet, Isaac. But let's see if you feel the same way after I explain what this is all about."

The warm breeze blew on my face as I kept my eyes straight ahead on the lights of the Berkeley fishing pier and Skates restaurant that sits like a landmark to the entrance of the Berkeley Marina. Her voice was soft and soothing, and despite what she was saying, her words flowed over me like a warm blanket.

"Well, Isaac, I already explained why I left China. Uncle Peter seemed secure for a while. He was a hero of the Long March and a major in the Army. He had many friends and allies high up in the Party. But what you have to know is that Uncle Peter was under the command of Comrade Lin Biao during the War of Liberation. I don't know how much you know about China, and I hope I don't sound too much like a history teacher, but you have to know these things for you to understand."

I smiled at her. "But, you are a teacher, aren't you?"

"Well, yes. But then, I don't usually make love to my students."

"Or nearly get them killed."

"Can't say I didn't warn you."

It was a long explanation, something about this fellow Lin having a falling out with Mao over the Cultural Revolution and him ending up dead in a suspicious airplane crash. Then the purges in the Red Army began. That's when Peter Wu headed for the nearest exit, and ended up in Oakland.

"Uncle Peter settled down here in America," she said. "He enjoyed his job at the hotel, and he was well respected in the community because everyone knew who he really was. But I believe he missed home."

"Yes, a friend of mine, whose father is a big *macher* in

Chinatown, told me about Peter."

"What's is that...*macher*, Isaac?"

"Mucky muck, an important person. It's Yiddish."

"Really, who?"

"Johnny Wong. His old man is head of the Chinese Merchants Association, or something like that."

"Oh sure. Everybody knows Johnny Wong. He flirts with all the woman."

"Did he flirt with you?"

"Sure, but it was all just kidding around. My uncle was good friends with his father. But anyway, Isaac; I thought everything was fine until about three years ago when this man came to our house. He was this young guy with funny sunglasses. Very, how you say, cool looking?"

"Oh shit." I remembered the business card in my pocket and pulled it out and showed it to her. "Is this the guy?"

"Isaac, where did you get this?"

I told her about my run in with the Ray-Ban guy; that he had been watching her house and my encounter with him earlier that day.

"What's the card say?"

"Huang Xiabo, Attaché, Chinese Consulate, and the address of the Consulate here in San Francisco. He preferred to be called Rick. He said that was his American name. My uncle had been inquiring about returning to China since the Cultural Revolution had ended with Chairman Mao's death. That's what this Rick guy came to talk about. We were welcome to return to China, he said. Uncle Peter could return to the Red Army, and he would receive all back pay for the years he was self exiled in America. He said I would be given a position at Guangzhou University."

"Attaché, isn't that like our CIA guys attached to U.S. embassies?"

"Some of them, yes. It's the same in every Embassy. Basically

Isaac, they are spies working under the cover of diplomatic immunity. But since both sides know who they are it doesn't matter. He is probably Guóānbù, like your CIA."

"How do you know all this?" I asked, not really wanting to know.

"My uncle was head of security in our province. He knew everything, and told me about it after we came here. Anyway this Rick told Uncle Peter that he still had many friends and loyal comrades in the Army, and they would gladly have him back. Only then there was a condition..."

Just then the ship to shore radio squawked, interrupting her. "Hold on, I have to take this," I interrupted.

A voice came over the radio speaker:

*"This is the Berkeley Harbor Master calling the Pipe Dream. Over."*

"This is the Pipe dream, Isaac Smith skipper, over."

*"Isaac Smith. This isn't Smitty was a delegate at the Labor Council? Over."*

"One and the same, over"

*"Smitty, I was a delegate with SIU. You remember me? Mike. Over."*

"Mike Haggerty? Over"

*"One and the same, brother. What can I do for you? Over."*

"Request guest docking, over."

*"No problem, brother. End of Dock F. I'll send a man to help you tie up. Over."*

"Appreciated. Over."

*"Oh, and Smitty, if there's anything I can do for you just ask. You did my union a biggy getting support for our strike. And don't forget to report to the Marina office in the a.m. Over and out."*

I cut the engine speed down to five knots as we entered the marina.

"Whatever the catch to your story is, it'll have to wait until we tie up at the dock," I said, trying to act captain-like. I think she was amused.

She didn't have to be asked. As I approached the end of the dock she went to the bow and threw the mooring line to the man standing on the dock. I lined the boat up to the end of the dock and she stepped off as if she were a deck hand on a fishing boat. She secured the bow line and then the stern line. `

"All secure, captain."

"Thanks partner," I yelled down to the man on the dock.

I could see him ogling Mei.

"You got a hell of a mate there, skipper. Stop by the office in the morning." He shouted back, and then walked off down the dock into the dark.

"You're really sexy when you get serious," I said. "You were telling me about...."

She gave me a stern look, poured another shot of Stoli, and downed it.

"That was a long time ago. This is now, and Uncle Peter is dead because he was serving his country."

"So that was the catch?"

"Yes Isaac that was what you call the catch. The Embassy had an assignment for him. That was what this Rick guy told him. And now Uncle Peter is dead, and whoever it was is looking for me."

"And let me guess, you know why."

"Yes Isaac. I know why."

We looked at each other for a minute. I was waiting for an explanation that wasn't coming voluntarily.

"Well," I finally said. "Are you going to tell me?"

"Sweet Isaac. The more you know the more you're going to get dragged in. And it's really not your problem. This is Chinese business. I don't care what Uncle Peter asked you to do. You are *Gwailo*, non-Chinese."

I stood up. I was fed up with her attempts to brush me off. "Look, I did promise Peter, but that was my word to a dying man. That was before you made love to me. Chinese or not, I'm in this thing, and you're not going to change my mind. So, you can tell me what's going on or not, but I ain't going nowhere, and you're just stuck with me."

She stood up and put her arms around my neck and kissed me, pressing hers lips hard against mine and then pulled away and sighed, "Oh Isaac. What am I going to do with you?"

"What do you want to do with me?"

She kissed me again, this time gently, and then her lips slowly parted and accepted my eager tongue into the warmth of her mouth.

"Take me to bed and make love to me," she whispered

* * *

# CHAPTER 15

The morning sun streamed through the port like a blinding spotlight in my eyes, jarring me awake. The smell of brewing coffee drifted into the state room. I felt the spot where Mei-ling's body had clung next to me all night. She was gone. I eased myself out of the bed and reached for my robe. It was also gone, so I stepped into my pants, threw on a tee shirt and climbed the two steps into the salon.

Mei was standing in the small galley facing the coffee maker, wrapped in my terry cloth robe and looking far better in it than I did. She had two cups set up and I was instantly sorry I had gotten up, figuring she planned to bring it back to bed. She turned and saw me. I was right.

"Oh, you're up?"

"Well, I could go back to bed."

"No, no. You're up now. I made us coffee. You like something in it?"

"Just sugar, two."

I slid into the dinette. She brought the coffee over to me and sat down on the other side. For a minute we just sat there, me looking at her and remembering the night before. She just stared into her coffee, like she had something on her mind. I didn't want to know what it was, but I knew I would find out.

"I couldn't sleep all night, my darling Isaac," she finally said. "You are such a wonderful man, and I have grown quite fond of you over the past couple of days."

I could hear it coming.

"But I decided, you're going to have to, how did you say, throw me to the dogs..."

"Wolves. And no, I will never do that."

"You must, Isaac. I can't tell you what is going on, and you can't be involved."

"I'm already involved," I protested.

"No Isaac. I told you, this is Chinese business."

"I know that the Chinese Secret Service had assigned your uncle to do something. I know they asked you to take his place. And I know someone is trying to kill you. So, I'd say I know a lot."

"How'd you know they want me to take his place?" She seemed genuinely surprised, despite all that had happened.

"Because I read the note attached to that stuffed panda they gave you at the wake, or whatever you call it."

"How could you read it? It was in Chinese."

"I'm a quick study."

"Don't joke with me, Isaac."

"Sorry, I took it to Johnny and he read it for me."

"So you know I can't forget this thing. It's very important to the people of China. Besides, I will not let Uncle Peter's murderers get away with it."

She was obviously pissed off about me lifting the note.

"Look Mei. I'm in this thing. Not for the Chinese people, or even for you, but because I made a promise to a dying man who didn't deserve to die, and I plan on keeping that promise. I

82

told you that before and I meant it. I'm doing this because I have to. So you better get used to it."

She still refused to look at me, and sipped idly at her coffee. I could almost see her mind working over time. She finally looked up.

"Okay Isaac, I guess I can't discourage you. So, whatever you say."

"That's better," I said and put my hand on hers. She smiled but it wasn't sincere. She had something up her sleeve.

"I have to go to the Marina office and check in. You stay put. I may be gone for a while."

"Yes Isaac."

I felt uneasy as I made my way down the dock. She had given in far too easily. I had only known her for a couple of days, but long enough to know she was self-willed and brave to the point of foolishness. At least, that's what I thought. The passion she had shown, first the mixture of fear and excitement morphing into anonymous sex on the floor of her sitting room, and then the abandoned lovemaking aboard the boat. But, despite her affection, I couldn't really tell what was going on in her head. Inscrutable, wasn't that what they said about the Chinese? Or was it just a racist characteristic invented in Hollywood; Charlie Chan and all that shit. But I still didn't know what the fuck was going on. All I could do was try to keep close to her while she did what she was going to do. I would try to watch her back, and what a pretty back it was.

"Don't sweat the docking fee," the man, who identified himself as Skip, said from behind the counter. "The Harbor Master said it was on him. You must be a special dude, brother. The Harbor Master don't give no one a break."

He passed me a key to the dock gate.

"You got a phone I can use?"

"Sure," he said. "And by the way, there were a couple of shady looking Chinese gangster types asking about you and the lady."

"How do you know they were looking for me?" I said, guessing they were probably the same hoods hunting us at the restaurant.

"White guy and a Chinese sweetie? Pretty obvious. I told them nothing."

"Thanks. The phone?"

"Come around and you can use the one in the office."

I called the union and Marta answered.

"Any messages for me?"

"Yeah. There were a couple of cops looking for you. Said they needed a statement from you. Left their card and said you should call them. Also, that guy from the *Tribune's* been calling; said to tell you to call him as soon as I heard from you. So I'm telling you."

Sarcastic bitch. I got the number for the cops, hung up and dialed Ted's number at the *Trib*. He was in.

"Smitty where the hell you been?"

"I'm in Berkeley, on my boat in the marina."

"Well comrade, I don't know what you got yourself into this time, but you'd better meet me. I got some information I think you'd better hear."

It sounded serious. I agreed to meet him at Hs Lordships, the restaurant near the fishing pier. It was walking distance and my car was back in Emeryville.

I asked Skip if he had an extra watch cap I could borrow, just in case the hoods were waiting in the parking lot.

"Sure, here's an old one."

"I'll return it," I said, slipping it onto my head and down over my forehead and ears.

"Forget it, brother; I was going to toss it anyway."

I stepped out of the Marina office and looked around. The two hoods from the other night in Emeryville were slouched down in a black Lincoln Towncar, smoking cigarettes. They glanced in my direction, but I doubted they recognized me.

I stopped at the bait store and picked up some pastries to bring back to Mei for breakfast, wondering if she would still be pissed at me. It didn't take much to find out.

She was hunched over a cup of coffee studying what looked like a journal. She refused to look up or acknowledge my presence.

"I brought us some breakfast rolls," I said, and worked my way behind her into the galley for a cup of coffee, taking a snoop at the journal for all the good it did; it was written in Chinese. She had gotten dressed, wearing the same jeans, but with a light v-neck sweater. Her hair was up in a bun exposing her smooth neck. I wanted to lean over and kiss it, but feared the back of her hand would be my reception.

Instead I asked, "What's that?" and was surprised to get an answer.

"It was my Uncle Peter's."

"So, what's it say?"

"That is not your concern. But thanks for the pastries," she added.

I thought I caught the hint of a smile.

She took a bear claw and went back to studying the journal.

I sat down across from her with my coffee. She kept her head buried in the little book. It was obvious no matter what I said I wasn't going to find out what was so interesting. I stood up.

"I guess I'll go out for a few hours."

Still no response as she kept her nose in the book, so I walked to the cabin door and turned to her. "Please, stay put 'til I get back." I knew I should have told her about the two thugs in the parking lot, but I didn't want to alarm her.

She looked up from the journal. "Isaac, come here."

I walked back to the dinette. She took my hand and pulled

me toward her and kissed me.

"It could never work between us, Isaac," she sighed. "I wish it could."

There was something in the way she said it. It was like, so long chump, only in a loving sort of way.

"Please Mei, don't leave the boat."

She buried her head back in the journal.

* * *

# CHAPTER 16

It was more than an hour before I had to meet Ted, but I figured I could kill the time. It was another uncommonly beautiful day with a bright hot sun glaring down from over the East Bay Hills. It promised to be in the low eighties, a moderate summer day in most places, but a scorcher for the Bay Area, sending people stampeding to the parks and beaches.

I headed to Cesar Chavez Park on the north end of the man made peninsula that jutted out into the Bay. The park had been created out of what was the Berkeley dump. Now it was 96 acres of low hills and paths along the shoreline. From the rise you could see a 180 degree panorama of the entire Bay Area. I took it all for granted most of the time; most people who live here do. But once in awhile I would realize that it was one of the most impressive and scenic places in the world, and the view from an abandoned garbage dump rivaled any in the world.

I sat on one of the benches along the mile and a half walk encircling the park and lit a Lucky, letting the smoke fill my lungs. It was the Lake Merritt of Berkeley where people, young and old, walked and jogged. Dog lovers passed by with their canines in tow, and young couples pushed baby strollers. I wondered what my life might have been if I had taken another path. Would I be walking a dog? Perhaps a kid of my own, with a loving woman hanging on my arm. Perhaps not.

Time passed as I watched the sailboats taking advantage of the rare warm easterly breeze. It was picture postcard stuff. But it was time to move on. Reality—my reality—waited.

It was a little after twelve when I got back to the other side of the Marina. I checked the parking lot. The two hoods were stationed in the same place. Mei must have taken my advice and stayed put, so I headed toward the Fisherman's Pier that jutted out into the Bay and at one time extended out a mile serving as a ferry terminal. But it had been broken up long ago and now went out about a quarter of that distance and was used for exactly what it was named for. Skates was to the right and Hs. Lordships to the left. Skates was non-union. Hs. Lordships, union.

Hs. Lordships hadn't changed much since the 60's. It sat suspended over the water looking like it could slip into the Bay at anytime. But somehow it stayed put, no thanks to the owners who refused to put any money into it. I had been the BA there a number of years back. It was an easy house. The employees had been there so long they practically ran the place.

I found Ted sitting at the bar talking to the bartender. The place was nearly deserted; lunch wasn't big and most people went to Skates. Hs. Lordships' major business came from the upstairs banquet room, with its wall to wall windows offering the same views as the park, with a capacity seating of 500, along with three smaller spaces downstairs. There were also rooms for private parties, facilities Skates lacked.

"Can I get you a drink?" the young bartender asked.

I didn't recognize him, so I read his name tag.

"Hi Tom, my name's Smitty," I said. "I'm with the union."

His face dropped and he began to busily wipe down the bar.

"How long you been working here Tom?"

"'Bout a month," he said.

"You join the union yet?"

"Eh, no sir didn't know I had to."

"Smitty."

"Eh, no Mr. Smitty. I didn't know I had to."

"Just Smitty, and yeah, you have to. You want to work non-union, get a job at Skates. Dig?"

"Yes sir," he said meekly.

He knew he had to join the union. He just didn't want to put out the dough for the initiation fee.

"Good, I'll tell the office. They'll deduct your initiation and first month's dues from your pay check. Okay?"

"I guess."

"Let's grab a booth," I said to Ted, sliding off the bar stool.

"You were pretty tough on the kid, weren't you," Ted said as we settled down into the black leather seats overlooking the cove that was formed out of the southern boot of land the restaurant sat on.

"No, everyone bitches when it's time to join. But when they get into a jam, they come running."

"Can I get you fellas something?"

Marci was a tall red head. She was wearing a short black skirt and her long black net stocking legs were made all the more shapely by the high heels she wore. A white peasant blouse showed off her more than ample bust. She was a sexy broad approaching middle age; the type of gal I used to be attracted to before I met Mei-ling.

"Smitty, ain't seen you around here in awhile. You going to be our business agent again?"

"No," I said. "But it's good to see you Marci. How're the kids?

"Getting big, Smitty."

"You know, we fought hard so you wouldn't have to dress like that."

"I know, Smitty, but it's good for tips."

"Hmmm. This here's my friend Ted. He's a newspaper man."

"Do tell," Marci said, obviously not impressed. "What'll you gents have?"

I ordered a BLT and Coffee. Ted, a Shrimp Salad.

"So, what's this information you think I ought to know?"

He took a sip of water. "I shouldn't be telling you this, but this is my last warning to cut this lady friend of yours loss."

I took out a cigarette and lit up. "So?"

"Well, I got a call yesterday from a buddy of mine in the FBI working in the San Francisco office. Told me he heard I was interested in Peter Wu. Well, bottom line, what I told you I suspected was right. It seems your Mr. Wu was infiltrating a Chinese Triad from Guangdong province who're smuggling immigrants and dope, and god knows what else in from South China. He said the Bureau was out of the loop on the case; must be State Department. That's what he said anyway. I can't touch the story, but I can give you a last warning. These guys don't play, Smitty. They'll slit your throat soon as look at you."

"Is that all you can tell me?"

"That's it, but if you read the papers, you'd know about the dead immigrants found in the freight container in L. A. last week."

"Yeah, I saw an item in the *LA Times*."

"The *Times*, eh. I'm impressed. Well, anyway that's just one case of many. Seems someone's been tipping off the authorities, and my guy suspects it was Wu. Said they may have suspected Wu and murdered him in public to make an example of him."

90

Marci brought us our food. We ate in an uncomfortable silence. I had suddenly lost my appetite. I stared out at the wind surfers that filled the cove.

Ted finished his salad and stood up. I could see I was going to get stuck with the bill again.

"Look Smitty, if you can't drop this now, watch your back."

"I will."

"Here's my friend's card. He said you should contact him if you find out anything, and not to take any chances. Good advice from a pro." He handed me a business card.

"I thought you said the FBI wasn't involved?"

That's exactly why he wants to hear from you. I'd call him and see what he has to say if I were you. Oh, I'll catch the tab."

He must have been really worried if he offered to pay. He went to the cashier and then left. I pulled out a Lucky and looked at the business card:

### Gabriel Feinberg
### Special Agent
### Federal Bureau of Investigation

"Well, at least he was a Jewish Fed." I said to myself, but he was still FBI.

I finished my smoke, staring out at the sea of small sails swishing around the cove. I guess I should have been scared shitless, but for some reason I wasn't. Instead I just felt numb.

The sun light blinded me for a second as I stepped out of Hs Lordship's. Lunch had only been about an hour, but the temperature must have risen ten degrees. By the time I got back to the bait and tackle shop I was sweating. I checked the parking lot. The black Lincoln was gone. I figured they must have given up.

I was anxious to get back to the boat and check on Mei, hoping she had forgiven me. Perhaps even a little sex if I was lucky. But when I got to the end of the dock I got a strange empty feeling. I jumped on board and hit the cabin door calling her name. No answer. It didn't take much to search the boat. She was gone. But oddly, she had left her green night gown on the bed, as if she was leaving me a reminder of her. It worked. I picked it up and pressed it to my face, deeply inhaling the smell of her. Corny, but I wasn't in my right mind. I should never have left her alone.

I went back up to the salon. Under her half empty coffee cup was a note on top of the journal. I moved the journal and opened the note. It was written in perfect cursive:

*Sweet Isaac,*

*When you read this you will know that I have left. I know how much you want to protect me and that you made a promise to my uncle. But this is now my responsibility. I have grown very fond of you over these past few days, but I cannot drag you into this. I could never live with myself if anything happened to you.*

*Isaac, it seems our paths were meant to cross at this time, and perhaps our destinies lie in the same direction. But right now I must do something that is not your obligation. It is mine alone.*

*I am leaving Uncle Peter's journal with you for safe keeping and so that you will know that we will meet again.*

*I am yours fondly,*
*Mei-ling*

I sat there holding the letter. Why hadn't I told her about the two hoods in the parking lot. Now it was too late, and all I could do was hope she hadn't been snatched. I began to plot my next move, but came up blank.

\* \* \*

# CHAPTER 17

I decided to go back to Mei-ling's house, but first I wrapped the journal up in a sheet of canvas and stowed it in the engine compartment where it would be safe. I secured the cabin door with a pad lock. I figured that it was the journal the thugs were after, and they suspected rightly that Mei-ling had it. At least that's what I figured.

I got out into the parking lot and it occurred to me that my car was back in Emeryville. I wasn't thinking straight. I probably could have walked the four miles to the Emeryville Marina, but my sense of urgency drove me into the Marina Office. Skip was still standing behind the counter.

"What can I do for you now?" he asked.

"I need to call a cab, my car's back in Emeryville and I got to get somewhere quick."

"A cab? That will take a half hour if not longer. You must not use cabs often."

"How else can I get there, walk?"

"Too hot for that. I'll be happy to run you over there if you like."

"Really? That would be great," I said.

No problem. Any friend of the Harbor Master is a friend of mine. Angie," he called back to a woman in the small office, "Hold down the fort while I run this guy over to the Emeryville Marina."

I thought we'd get in his car and drive over, but instead he led me down to the dock behind the office. We got onto a twenty foot motor launch, the kind they used to cruise the harbor.

"Hop on," he said as he undid the docking line.

I was lucky he wasn't the inquisitive type; preferred talking about himself. The Honda outboard hummed as we cruised out to the breakwater at five knots, and then he opened it up. In the ten minutes it took to get to the Emeryville marina I learned that Skip had been a commercial fisherman. He had inherited a boat from his father. Fishing salmon was in his blood, but the rising cost of diesel, falling wholesale prices and diminishing fish stock forced him to sell his boat. It was a common story up and down the coast.

"It's the times," I said.

"Yeah, suppose so. Some guys are hanging in there, fishing crab and bottom fish, but I was only rigged for Salmon, and I couldn't raise the dough for the investment in crab pots and drag nets anyway. So here I am. Good gig with bennies. Can't complain, but I miss fishing."

He maneuvered the boat into the Emeryville Marina and slowly motored to the dock closest to the restaurant. I jumped off and thanked him.

"I don't know what you're into, brother, but you better watch your back. Chinese business should stay in Chinatown. Us honkies shouldn't nose in, if you get my drift."

I stood on the dock and watched as he maneuvered the launch out of the dock and back into the marina channel. His parting words echoed in my head. I got his drift all right, but I was caught in an undertow that kept pulling me in deeper.

It took only three turns around the block before a car pulled out from the curb leaving a valuable parking spot. I stopped to back in. A car horn immediately started blasting behind me. It was a VW bug. I looked in the rear view mirror and there was the same old Chinese guy who had blasted me the other day, waving his fist and shouting in Chinese which I was sure translated into, "get the fuck out of the way you round eyed prick."

I still had the key Mei had given me, but found the door was already open. Hope springs eternal and I rushed in expecting Mei to be there.

The place was just as I had left it, like a hurricane had swept through with shit scattered all over the floor. I called her name, but no answer. I pushed open the door leading to the kitchen. "Mei?"

"I was expecting you."

It was the Ray-Ban guy, sitting at the kitchen table with a cup of steaming coffee and an automatic pistol in front of him.

"What the fuck are you doing here? Where's Mei-ling?" I said with the most authoritative voice I could muster.

"Shit man, I was hoping you could tell me. Sit down. Let's talk."

"Why don't you ask your two buddies in the Black Lincoln?"

He put his hand on the gun. "Sit down, Smitty. Have a cup of coffee with me. I do like coffee better than tea. Odd for a Chinese don't you think?"

I reMeined standing. "Fuck you Rick, or whatever your name is."

"So, Mei-ling told you who I am. Then you know I am not some kind of gangster like those two hoods. Why don't you try to be a little friendlier?"

"Why should I trust you?"

"Because I'm the good guy, that's why. Now sit the fuck down." He fidgeted with the gun.

I pulled out a chair, turned it around and straddled it.

"Yeah, that's why you forced Peter into spying for you before he could be repatriated home. I don't call that being a good guy."

"For your information Major Wu was pleased to take the assignment. He is a patriot and an officer in the People's Liberation Army. It was his duty."

"And it got him killed."

"Yes, regrettably. But he will be honored as a hero of the Chinese People. Now let me get you a cup of coffee. I just brewed it. Mei-ling doesn't have the best taste in coffee, but it will do. Personally, I prefer Peets. You know it? My favorite. You Americans have pretty good joe. That's what they call it, correct?"

"Among other things. I'll pass thanks. How the fuck do you speak such good English anyway?"

"Moved here in 1972. Went to Galileo High in San Francisco for a year, then UC Berkeley, Class of '79."

"Then why the hell are you working for the Chinese government?"

He laughed. It was all a big joke.

"I'm Chinese. My government sent me here to learn how to be American. You see, I was groomed from an early age to work for the government. We Chinese plan ahead, unlike you Americans. You go for the big bucks today without a thought for tomorrow. Some day we will be number one in the world because we plan ahead."

He had a point. American stores were already filling with goods "made in China." U.S. factories were closing left and right and moving anywhere they could find cheap labor and China was happy to provide it.

He took out a cigarette and lit it with a gold lighter that had a picture of Mao and played a musical tune which I guessed was some Chinese Revolutionary song. He blew out a cloud of smoke, and looked at the lighter. "Pretty cool, eh? Got it in Hong Kong. You want one? I can get it for you?"

"No thanks."

He put the lighter into his coat pocket. "So, you like that Chinese pussy; good enough to get killed for, eh? Me, I prefer your American chicks. They're, how you say, kinky. You know?"

I had had enough from this joker. I stood up. "Look pal, you'd better get the fuck out of here before I call the cops. Breaking and entering's a crime in America."

"You forget, I'm employee of Chinese Consulate; Diplomatic immunity." He said smugly.

"Yeah, well the Oakland cops don't give a shit if you're Mao Tse-tung. They'll throw you in the city jail with a bunch of gang bangers until your consulate gets you out, and you don't want to be in there."

He took a sip of the coffee and dropped his cigarette into the cup. "You're probably right amigo." He slipped the gun into his coat pocket. "I guess I'll be on my way. But we'll meet up again."

He started to walk to the door and then stopped and turned to face me. "By the way, you didn't happen to notice if Mei-ling had a book, a kind of journal, did you?"

I shook my head in the negative, but I knew that he knew I was lying.

"Well, if you happen to run across it...." He hesitated for a moment, and then walked out, slipping his Ray-Bans over his eyes.

I sat there frozen until I heard the front door shut.

* * *

# CHAPTER 18

"You're the only friend I got, Johnny"

"I'm the only friend you got speaks Chinese."

I stared at the glass of bourbon in front of me. The Oaks was filling up as gamblers settled in for the afternoon. The bar was still relatively empty. Most of the business was being handled by a young Chinese woman service bartender who must have been new. I didn't have to worry about her union status. Johnny would take care of that. He had greeted me with a sarcastic, "I see you're still alive, Smitty."

"Come on Johnny, just come down to my boat after you get off."

He crossed his arms on the bar and leaned toward me while glancing back at the new bartender to be sure she was busy and not listening. "Look Smitty, a Chinese fuck around in Triad business, he end up in tomorrow's Kung Pao chicken."

"Come on, Johnny, your father's a big wig in Chinatown;

who's going to mess with you."

"You don't get it; these Chinese Triads, they could give a shit about us American Chinese. My pop is small bananas."

"Well, just think it over. I got nowhere else to turn," I said, hoping my desperation would convince him. "If you decide to come just ask the guy at the Marina office. His name's Skip. I'll tell him to let you in the gate. I'm at the end of F dock." I gulped down the JD and put a fiver on the bar. "Think it over Johnny. I really need your help."

I slid off the stool and walked out of the Oaks into the noon sunshine.

I checked the clock in the nautical trio on the wall. It was four. The barometer noted fair weather and the thermometer weighed in at 80 degrees Fahrenheit. Since Johnny got off at two, I figured he had decided to opt out. I couldn't blame him. I'd probably do the same.

Then, I heard my name being called from the dock. I took a look. It was Johnny, being escorted by Skip. I came out of the cabin.

"This fellow says he's a friend of yours," Skip said.

"He's cool," I answered.

"Sorry Pal," Skip said to Johnny. "Can't take any chances."

Johnny climbed on board.

"Thanks Skip," I said.

"No a problem." Skip answered and turned to walk back down the dock.

I went below. Johnny was sitting at the dinette.

"You're going to get me killed," he said out of breath. "Give me a goddamn drink, will you."

I poured him a glass of Stoli. I had seen him sneak a shot of vodka on the sly at the Oaks and figured it was his drink. He gulped it down.

"Who was that asshole?" he said. "Some kinda racist or something?"

"No, Skip's okay, but we've had a couple of Chinese gangsters hanging around and he wasn't taking no chances."

"Gangsters?"

I could see the worry on his face.

"Don't worry brother. They're gone."

"Now, what the fuck is this thing you need me to read? I want to get this over with and get the hell out of here."

I fetched the journal from the engine compartment and dropped it on the table in front of him.

"It was Peter's. I need to know what's in it. It could be a matter of life and death."

"Whose life, yours? Certainly not mine. You wouldn't have gotten me involved if you were concerned about my life. I don't even know why I came."

"Look Johnny, I wouldn't have asked you to come if it wasn't important. Mei-ling's life is in danger, and I think I might be able to help her if I know what's in this book."

He looked up. "Peter's niece? I thought she was with you."

"She was. But she left and I'm worried those hoods might have snatched her."

He fingered the journal for a minute. Then he opened it.

"I might be able to read this. But I have to warn you Smitty, I fucked off a lot in Chinese School, and it was a long time ago. I can read menus okay and an occasional newspaper, only..."

"Only what?"

"Only this is hand written. I read Chinese in print; ditched the calligraphy class."

"Well, just read what you can. Maybe that will be enough," I said, pouring myself a glass of Jack and refilling his glass with the Stoli.

He buried his face in the journal like he was being sucked

into it. "Give me one of your cigarettes," he demanded with his eyes glued to the journal with his hand out to receive a Lucky.

"Let me see. This first entry is from nearly two years ago. You want me to read that?"

"Well, let's see what it says."

He looked it over a minute. "Give me a light, Smitty." He seemed to be getting a kick out having me wait on him for a change. He took a long drag without looking up and blew a cloud of blue smoke out of the side of his mouth so as not to blur the page. He finally looked up. "Shit Smitty, this don't sound like the Peter I knew for years. I'll have to give you an idea of what it says. Chinese language isn't like English. If I translate directly it wouldn't make any sense."

"Just fucking read," I insisted.

It was pretty obvious Johnny wasn't real confident. He probably understood it, but he was not a translator, so he kind of explained what it said.

What I understood from what he said was that Peter was honored to once again serve the Chinese Peoples' Revolution—the Ray-Ban guy from the Consulate was right, as much as I hated to admit it. It was as if all of his years in the U.S. had no meaning for Peter. I wondered if it was the same for Mei-ling; if she was just sort of hanging out in America until she could go back to China.

Johnny went on interpreting in his own words. Apparently this agent named Huang Xiabo at the Consulate had given him the locations where he could best contact a New York Tong working the West Coast. The Ghost Shadows, they called themselves and they were working with one of the Triads that were expanding into America and Europe. He spread the word that he was in need of a lot of money and was desperate.

It took a couple of weeks before he was contacted by a man named Li Pang. According to Peter, he was dressed a lot like my buddy from the Consulate, but the Ray-Bans couldn't hide a pock marked face and a scar down his rutty cheek. Peter's training as an intelligence agent hadn't gone to waste. He noted every detail. This Pang guy came into the Hyatt Bar one morning, ordered a beer, handed Peter a piece of paper and left without paying. Only a bartender would make note of that detail.

Peter ended up at a *Xiangqi* club in an alley off Stockton Street in San Francisco's Chinatown. Several dozen old men sat at tables playing, smoking and pondering over game boards with hand-carved Chinese pieces in front of them.

Johnny looked up. "*Xiangqi* is a kind of Chinese Chess, Smitty, only more complicated than the Western game; same principle; a game of war."

Li sat at one of the tables and invited him to play. Peter evidently was a master *Xiangqi* player and had won many tournaments in China. He beat Li easily. That's when a fat man with wire rim glasses and a cigarette dangling from his mouth came over and bowed slightly, saying how honored he was to meet the famous Major Ching-Shu Wu. It seems the quick defeat of Li had convinced the man that Peter was who he said he was. The fat man escorted him into an office in the back of the club, and then settled behind a cluttered desk. Peter noted that the place smelled of stale cabbage, cooking oil and cigarettes. The fat man introduced himself as Wang Ho Lee.

Peter told the fat man that he still had many contacts in Guangdong Province, both in the Red Army and among Communist administrators, facts that he was sure Wang already knew. Many of these men, like Peter, had become disillusioned during the Cultural Revolution and believed they had been treated disrespectfully. Now that Mao was dead along with his Cultural Revolution they were out to make as much money as possible. They knew that with the death of Mao a new era of economic freedom was coming to China, and they wanted to get their piece. Peter said he planned to return soon, and didn't want to go back broke.

"Well, Peter must have been convincing, because this Wang guy told him a shipment was passing through the port of Guangzhou." Johnny said. "Apparently they had problems with the authorities. He notes that the officials and cops were probably arresting the smugglers and pocketing any money or drugs they found. If there were hopeful immigrants, they would be robbed and also arrested."

Johnny had his face buried in the journal as he puffed clouds of smoke from his cigarette. The more he read the more absorbed he seemed to get.

"Peter says he was being tested, but it was his in to the gang. He agreed to make his contacts, telling Wang he'd have to make it worth their while. The fat man assured him it would be. After the meeting Peter informed Huang at the Consulate, and then contacted a General friend of his in Guangzhou city and made the arrangements. The shipment was allowed to pass through the port. He had told his General buddy to be sure and stop it, and then let it go unmolested, so they would know the fix was in."

Johnny smashed the remnants of his cigarette out. "Do you believe this shit, Smitty? It reads like a—what's his name—le Carrè novel."

It was all pretty much what I already knew, but I was looking for something that might lead me to Mei-ling. I offered Johnny another cigarette and poured us both another drink.

"Who would have ever expected Peter Wu?" Johnny said,

"Skip to the back and let's see what happened, maybe why Peter was murdered." I lit Johnny's cigarette.

"No man, this is interesting shit."

Johnny's earlier rush to leave had vanished.

"Come on, Johnny. It'll take you all night to read the whole thing."

"Well, okay. I'm expected for dinner anyway, and my pop don't like us to be late..."

He thumbed through to the back pages and studied them for a moment, and then offered his interpretation.

"After more than a year and a half the gang was beginning to think Peter had been snitching on them. Someone told them the cops were being tipped off. They tried to eliminate any evidence, and killed a few freight containers full of immigrants. Say, I remember reading something about that."

"Yeah, me too. Just read, Johnny."

"Jesus, Smitty, don't be an asshole about it. I could be risking my life doing this for you."

If he was trying to make me feel guilty, he succeeded and I apologized. Johnny returned to the journal.

Suspicion or no, Wang still had one more job for him; a valuable shipment, unlike the usual illegal immigrants and drugs. It was important it got through without any interference. He would double the usual payoff if it reached the waiting freighter safely.

Johnny went silent. He studied the journal like it was the racing form for Golden Gates Race Track.

"Well?" I said.

He looked up at me. "Apparently this was the shipment Peter and his buddies at the Consulate were waiting for. Peter doesn't say what it was, but it had to be something very important to the Chinese Government, that's for goddamn sure. I'd bet the gangsters knew that, so they made sure Peter made the arrangements and then blew him away before he could tell his buddy at the Consulate. That's what I'd bet."

It made sense.

"I wouldn't bet against you." I said. But it still didn't give me any clues as to where Mei-ling was. "Is there nothing more?"

Just a note here on the last page. Ridge Road end...whatever that means?"

"Let me see," I said, taking the journal from him. It was written in English, as if it was just a reminder to himself.

"I have to go," Johnny said, standing up. "I'm already late, and my father will give me hell."

He gulped down the last of his vodka and snuffed the cigarette out. "How do you smoke these things?"

"Habit," I said. "I'll walk you back to your car."

"No thanks, Smitty. I'd rather not be seen with you if it's all the same."

"Sure. I know it took a lot for you to come. I owe you."

"Just get those bastards that killed Peter before they get you. If not, well, I'll come to your funeral."

He disappeared out of the cabin. He had played it cool at the end, but I could tell he was scared shitless. I guess I should have been too.

I picked up the journal and flipped to the last page. *Ridge Road End.* It must have been important. I tore out the page, stuffed it into my pocket, and then wrapped the journal back up and returned it to its hiding place.

\* \* \*

# CHAPTER 19

I woke up hungry the next day. It was still early and I remembered I hadn't eaten anything the night before. I decided to go to the Oaks. I could get breakfast there, and I wanted to check and see how Johnny was doing. He had been pretty shook up when he left the day before.

I knew right away something was wrong when I didn't see him behind the bar. As far as I knew, he had never missed a day's work in ten years.

The Chinese lady was handling the entire bar. I asked her where Johnny was.

"Johnny, he in hospital," she said. "Stick me with whole bar," as if Johnny was in the hospital just to inconvenience her.

"What happened?"

"Don't ask me. Ask in office," she said pointing toward a door in the back of the Hof Brau.

*

Megan was a good looker, with body to match; she had probably been hired because of it. But she had proven to be a top notch secretary and book-keeper. Now, she practically ran the place while her bosses were out playing big shots.

"His cousin called early this morning. He said Johnny was at Kaiser Hospital and he didn't know when he'd be able to return to work."

"Did he say what happened and how he was?"

"Something about being mugged last night. That's all. Fucking Oakland, nobodies safe."

"Kaiser?"

"That's what he said, Smitty. If you see him, tell him I'll mail him his check."

He didn't have to worry about his job. He was protected by the union contract and Megan knew it.

"Oh, Smitty," she called as I headed for the door. "Tell him to get better and hurry back."

Breakfast would have to wait. I went out into the parking lot, got in my car and headed into Oakland.


Oakland Kaiser was a large boxy gray building with twin gray parking structures across the street; examples of 1950's functional architecture. I pulled into the parking structure and took my ticket. I hated having to pay to park. It was suppose to be a non-profit, but you couldn't prove it by me.

I entered the hospital at the MacArthur Boulevard side. An older black lady at the information desk told me Johnny was admitted at eleven the night before. He was now in ICU. She directed me to the elevators.

I got off on the third floor and went to the nurses' station to ask how Johnny was. The young black nurse gave me attitude when I asked. .

"He's in ICU. How do you think he's doing?"

"What happened to him?"

"We're not allowed to give out patient information accept to family. And you sure don't look like family. If you know how to speak Chinese maybe someone in that gang that's been here all night can tell you."

I started down the hall.

"And tell them there's no smoking in the waiting room," the nurse shouted after me.

The gang, as she called them, was huddled around the waiting room. A cloud of cigarette smoke hung heavy in the air. I guessed it was the Wong clan. One of them walked over to me. He looked a lot like Johnny.

"Hi. You must be Johnny's union guy." He said, holding out his hand to me.

I shook it. "Smitty. You his brother?

"No, cousin. The one with the pork bow shop. Johnny's told me about you."

"What happened? Is he all right?"

"Broken ribs, possible concussion and a broken leg. He got beaten up pretty bad. We figure it was one of the punk gangs that hang around his apartment building."

"Damn, that's terrible," I said; only I didn't buy the gang shit. It had to be the Chinese gangsters that had been hanging around the Marina, and that made it my fault he was in the hospital.

"They aren't letting anyone in to see him. But we're staying with my uncle and auntie. They're refusing to leave. I'm on my way to get food and tea for everyone. The only thing they got up here are vending machines."

There wasn't anything I could do there, so I went back down to the lobby with Johnny's cousin. Johnny had told him all about my involvement with Mei-ling and the Ghost Shadows at dinner the night before. He left me with the usual warning:

"Better stay clear, Smitty. Chinese business should stay in Chinatown. They don't like Caucasians nosing in."

I left him in the lobby and went to the phone booth. It was time to call Ted's buddy at the FBI. We made arrangements to meet.

* * *

# CHAPTER 20

We met at the second floor cafeteria of the Federal Building in San Francisco. I had told Feinberg I thought I was being followed. He said if they were Chinese gang members they wouldn't follow me into the Federal Building, and insisted I call him Gabe.

He was a balding, middle aged man, with what hair he did have pulled back in a tight pony tail; not at all what I had grown up believing FBI agents looked like. The FBI of my youth wore fedoras and gray overcoats; people to fear and hate. This guy was unironed white shirt with a loose neck tie decorated with a hula girl. The shoulder holster and gun he wore looked out of place.

We got coffee and sat at a small table in the back of the cafeteria.

"So, from what Ted tells me you've gotten yourself involved in some heavy shit," he said with a mild Brooklyn accent.

"Yeah, but let me ask you a question first?" I said, trying to get a feel for the guy.

"That's fair," he said.

"How the hell does a Jewish kid from Brooklyn end up in the FBI?"

"Queens actually. And to answer your question, I grew up in an orthodox family; Hebrew School, bar mitzvah, trips to Israel, the whole shmeer. When I graduated university with a Masters Degree in Criminology and Interrogation Techniques..."

"They have such a thing?" I interrupted.

"You'd be surprised what is offered," he said. "Anyway, I enlisted for Vietnam and ended up as an investigator with the Military police. That's where I met Ted. I was investigating a series of murders of Vietnamese prostitutes and he was interested in the story. We met for beers nearly every day, and became friends. After the war I went to Israel and joined the Mossad where I thought I could do something worthwhile after the shit in Nam. I received some good training there, but once in the field I couldn't stomach their methods. Besides, I was never really accepted by the Israeli agents, especially since I kept slipping into Yiddish which they looked down on. I had never paid much attention in Hebrew class. Anyway, I got fed up and quit. When I returned to the States I was recruited by the FBI, and here I am. Ted and I stayed in touch. Any more questions?"

"No," I said.

"You must be Jewish, Smitty" he said.

"What makes you think so?"

"Because only a Jew would ask such a stupid question."

We both laughed. Feinberg was okay in my book, even if he was a Fed.

"So, you want to know my story?" I asked.

"What's to know? Born in New York to Communist parents. Moved to L.A. at twelve. Roamed around the country for a while after high school flirting with various radical political movements, and doing a lot of drugs. Got a job as a bartender, and ended up working for a union. Pretty text book if you ask me."

"Shit, you guys got files on everyone?" I said.

"Actually, Ted told me about you. But I'll guess there's a file on you somewhere."

"Thank God. I would have felt slighted if there wasn't."

"So Izzy. You don't mind if a call you Izzy?"

"My Uncle called me Izzy. Most people call me Smitty."

"Yeah. I had a friend in New York named Izzy; died from an overdose. I'll call you Izzy."

"I'd prefer if you call me Smitty."

He took a sip of coffee. The small talk was over. He got right to the point:

"So, Izzy, what's a nice Jewish boy like you doing getting mixed up with a Chinese lady spy anyway?"

"Is she a spy? Funny, I never thought of Mei-ling that way."

"Izzy. She's working for the Chinese Government in the United States. What else could she be?"

"I asked you to call me Smitty."

"Okay Izzy. So?"

"I made a promise," I said, and give him a brief account of what had happened since Peter had been shot down at the Hyatt, leaving out a lot of the particulars. I didn't mention the journal because I knew he'd want to see it. So, I told him some of what I had learned from it.

Feinberg had taken out a note pad and was jotting down something.

"So, what's your involvement in all this?' I asked.

He explained that he was in the Organized Crime Unit investigating gang activity in New York's Chinatown. When they received information that the Ghost Shadow Tong had expanded to the West Coast, and was acting on behalf of a Chinese Triad, he and his partner were sent out to investigate. He thought Peter's death might be connected to the Tong, but when he went to investigate he was told by his superiors to leave it alone.

"I got the same message that our friend Ted got from his

editor; hands off," he said.

"But you're pursuing it anyway?"

"I was investigating the Ghost Shadows in New York for two years. I have a lot invested in this investigation. So, when Ted told me about you, I figured you'd probably need my help at some point. Seems I was right."

"So, I'm your ticket back into the investigation?"

"Something like that," he said.

I stared down into my half empty cup. Farmers Brothers—typical institution coffee.

"Well Feinberg?"

"Gabe."

"Well Agent Feinberg, how can you help me find Mei-ling?" I said, and pulled out a Lucky and lit up, wondering why I had bothered calling him in the first place.

"You never know," he said.

"Tell me something. If the Chinese are so interested in this so-called special shipment, why didn't they just stop it when it was coming down the river?"

Feinberg looked up from his note pad.

"Hmmmm. I'd guess it was something they didn't want discovered in China; something that might be embarrassing for them. So they must have worked out a deal with our State Department to operate here. It would be a win win situation for us; the Chinese bust up a criminal smuggling operation on American soil, and they owe us a favor. Only problem is, the gang must have bumped off your buddy, Peter Wu, before he could report back. Anyway, that's my theory."

"So, you're back to square one," I said.

"Well, not exactly. I have you."

I dropped by cigarette in the coffee, and stood up.

"I'm glad I could help you, Feinberg. But I still don't know where to start looking for Mei-ling."

He smiled up at me. "You're kind of fond of this gal, eh? I

find these Asian women attractive myself, only I got a wife and kids up in the Catskills for the summer, and she'd cut my balls off and put them in stuffed cabbage if she found me fooling around."

"So, you got any ideas?" I said, ready to walk out with as little information as I had walking in.

"If I were you, I'd start by going to the campus where she taught and ask around. Maybe she's been in contact with someone there. In the meantime, Izzy, you keep in touch."

He jotted something down on a blank sheet in his note pad, ripped it out and handed it to me.

"It's my pager; call anytime, night or day."

\* \* \*

# CHAPTER 21

I got off the freeway at the University Avenue exit, and headed for the UC Campus. I should have thought to check there myself. I guess that's the difference between an FBI investigator and a union business agent; figuring all the angles.

Finding a parking place around the campus is as hard as it is in Chinatown. I drove around for twenty minutes before finding a spot. As I started to back in I heard the sound of a Volkswagen horn. Shit, the old Chinese guy's followed me all the way to Berkeley. I looked in the rearview mirror. It was a VW bus and not my nemesis from Chinatown but a long haired hippy. I stuck my arm out the window and flashed the peace sign. He drove past me, his middle finger sticking in the air. Things had certainly changed since the 70's.

I walked onto Sprawl Plaza and saw a guy selling the Maoist newspaper of the Revolutionary Communist Party. I remembered them from when I was working near the campus in the early seventies when I had first met Ted and his Maoist buddy, Tommy Takamoto. Who better to ask where the Asian Studies Department was then a Maoist. Instead I got a blank look.

"You want to buy a paper, man?"

"No..."

He went into a spiel about the coming proletariat revolution when a young Chinese couple came up and saved me.

"We overheard that you are looking for the Asian Studies Department," the girl said.

I pulled away from the paper hustler.

"Thanks. Yeah. You know where it is?"

"Sure. It's in Dwinelle Hall, right over there."

"You kids in Asian Studies."

"No," she laughed. "We're in Business Administration. No money in Asian Studies."

She grabbed her friend's hand and they walked off.


The office of the Department head was on the third floor. Franklin D. Rabinski was in. A Jewish guy running the Asian Studies Department? I'd have to ask him about that.

Rabinski, sitting at a big desk surrounded by over-stuffed book cases, was nothing like what I expected. His thick black hair had traces of silver streaked through it. I guessed him to be in his fifties. His face was Asian, with dark wide set olive shaped eyes and a wispy gray beard. The only feature close to giving away his Semitic blood was his nose that seemed shaped especially to hold up his thick glasses. I handed him my card.

After inspecting it like it was a term paper, he looked up: "So, what can I do for you, Mr. Smith.? If your recruiting kitchen help, you've come to the wrong place," he said flatly.

"No, nothing like that. I'm trying to get some information on Mei-ling Wu. I believe she is a student here."

116

"Mei-ling?" He took off his glasses. He appeared to get misty eyed for a moment, as if the mention of her name hit a sensitive spot. I figured an affair at some point that ended badly … for him.

"What do you want with Mei-ling?" he asked.

"I was a friend of her uncle's."

He recovered his composure and replaced his glasses.

"Oh, yes, I read about him in the newspaper. Horrible thing!"

"Well, now she has disappeared and I'm trying to find her."

"Disappeared?" His face showed concern. "Have the police been notified?"

"The police can't be brought into this. It's urgent that I find her."

"Well, she is a student here, and a lecturer. She's working on her doctorate. She's a very bright woman, Mei-ling."

"Have you any idea where she might be?" I asked hopefully.

"I'm sorry, Mr. Smith, but as you can see, its summer break. I haven't seen her since June. However, you might ask Miss Banerjii. She teaches Southeast Asian history. They are good friends. I believe she's in her office today. Room 301."

"Thanks," I said, and headed for the door.

"Oh, Mr. Smith. If you find her let me know, would you. I am quite fond on Miss Wu."

"No problem. Oh, by the way; I was just curious; how come you have a Jewish name."

He laughed. "Why, don't I look Jewish?"

I knew it was a stupid question and his answer made me laugh. "I'm sorry, I just wondered."

"Well, it's simple really. My father escaped from the Nazis in 1939 and ended up in China. He married my mother there, and I'm the result. Does that satisfy your curiosity, Mr. Smith. You must also be a Jew." He said.

"What makes you say so?"

"Because, only a Jew would ask."

I turned and walked out the door, feeling a bit foolish.

Miss Banerjii was a good looking woman, with skin the color of smooth mahogany and large eyes to match. Her shiny black hair was in a pleated braid that hung down to her waist. When she rose to shake my hand her tight jeans gave away a sexy body which she tried to conceal under a loose fitting Cal tee shirt. A caste mark on her forehead stood out like a sign saying "Yes, I am Indian, stupid."

"Mr. Smith, how nice to meet you," she said cordially. There was a trace of an Indian accent which gave her voice a soft pleasant lilt. "Mei-ling has told me so much about you."

"Then you've seen her recently?"

"Please, sit down."

I pulled up a chair. "Where is she?" I asked, trying not to sound overly anxious.

"She's been staying with me for the past couple of days," she said, as she settled back behind her desk. "She said you might come around looking for her."

"Then she's alright?"

"Why yes, Mr. Smith."

"Please, call me Smitty. Everyone does."

"Smitty, then. I am Indira, but my friends call me Indy, like your Indiana Jones," she laughed. "Yes, she's quite well. Mei-ling and I have been friends for years. We both came to the Asian Studies Department at the same time."

"Well, I don't know what she's told you, Miss Banerjii."

"Indy," she corrected.

"Indy. Didn't Indiana Jones go around killing people of color?" I commented. I thought she'd appreciate that.

"Yes, that's why it is funny."

"Well, Indy, I don't know how much she has told you, but you must know her uncle was gunned down not long ago."

"Yes, I read about it in the paper. It was very sad. I liked Mr. Wu."

"But did she tell you that the same people who shot her uncle down are now gunning for her?"

A concerned look crossed her face.

"No Mr. Smith. She didn't convey that to me. Are you quite sure this is true? She only said she didn't want to stay in the house she shared with her uncle because it was too hard on her, and she just wanted to get away from everything."

"Well, I'm telling you, her life is in danger. And by staying with you she could be putting you in danger."

"Oh Mr. Smith, I am sure you must be exaggerating."

"Look, here's a phone number where I can be reached this evening. Have her call me," I insisted, jotting the number to the apartment on the flip side of my card and handing it to her.

"Well, I can't guarantee she will call, but I will give it to her," she said.

I extended my hand. "It's been nice meeting you, Ms. Banerjii."

"She stood up and took my hand. "Indy."

"Indy."

* * *

# CHAPTER 22

I hadn't been to the apartment for awhile. The calmness of Lake Merritt seemed oddly disturbing and made me restless. My life seemed to have been caught up in a whirlwind since that bloody day in the Hyatt basement. I unlocked the door only to find it chained on the other side.

"Smitty, is that you?"

It was Dede. She must have come home from Arkansas. I heard the chain slid open from the door and was greeted with a hug. I had forgotten how warm and sensual her body was until she pressed up against me. The heat radiated from her through the baggy cotton sweat suit she was wearing. For a moment I forgot about everything that had happened.

Then she pulled away from me.

"Where the fuck have you been? I've called your office three times, and all I get is some rude bitch telling me you'd taken time off."

I looked around. "Where's Chanel?"

"Don't ignore me, Smitty. Where have you been?" she said, refusing to be side tracked.

"It's a long story, honey. Where's my girl?"

I had grown fond of Chanel, taking her to the park or walks around the lake when her mother was studying.

"I left her with my Uncle and Aunt at the farm. I thought it would be good for her to spend some time in the country before going back for school. Besides, I have a research paper I have to finish up before the fall semester starts, and I won't have time for her. Now tell me, where have you been?"

"I need a drink," I said, walking over to the cupboard where I had stashed a bottle of Jack Daniels.

Dede followed me into the kitchen. She stood there with her arms folded as I poured a glass of whiskey.

"So?"

"Let me sit down and catch my breath," I said, and dropped into a kitchen chair.

She stood over me like a rabbi staring down at a student who had failed to study his Talmud. I took a drink and pulled out a Lucky. I suddenly felt exhausted as the events of the past few days caught up to me. I looked up into her beautiful bronze face with her large brown eyes fixed on me. I proceeded to tell her everything that had happened since Peter was shot down at the Hyatt. When I had finished I felt relieved.

"You really love this lady, Smitty," Dede finally said, not as a question, but affirming what she had heard. There wasn't a note of jealousy in her voice, only honest concern. I took a sip of Jack and thought about it for a moment.

"I'm not sure now," I said, and I suddenly felt very sad. "All I know is I made a promise to a dying man, and I have to keep my word."

She cradled my head in her bosom. "I know, baby, you're only doing what you believe is the right thing."

*

The smell of frying chicken filled the apartment as Dede cooked us dinner. She made the best fried chicken I had ever eaten, and I always eat too much of it. She said she learned how to cook from her grandmother who had learned from her mother back in Arkansas. She brought two plates into the living room and set them on the coffee table. There was fresh corn on the cob and collard greens. But even with the food sitting in front of me, I didn't have much of an appetite, as I sat on the couch, sipping Jack waiting for the telephone to ring.

Dede switched on the TV. The A's were playing, but even with the sluggers Conseco, McGuire and Henderson still on the roster, they were nowhere close to the World Series winning season in '89. But it was enough for me to space out and nibble at my food.

"I'm sorry, baby. I just don't feel like eating."

"It's alright. I understand," she smiled.

I must have dozed off, because the last thing I remember was Dede kissing me on the cheek and turning the TV off. The next thing I knew the phone rang, pulling me out of a deep sleep.

"Smitty, it's Indy," the voice on the other end said.

"Huh?" I forced myself to wake up.

"Indira. Mei-ling's friend." Her soft voice had the typical British reserve, but couldn't mask a sense of urgency. "Smitty, someone has broken into my apartment and Mei-ling is gone."

"Wait a minute," I said. "Slow down for a minute and tell me what happened."

"I went out. I had a date, and I left Mei-ling at home. I gave her your number and told her you wanted her to ring you up. Did she?"

"No."

"When I came home, the apartment was all topsy-turvy, like someone had been searching for something. I called the police, but they said there weren't any officers available, and I would have to wait until morning. When I told them about Mei-ling they told me I'd have to go down to police headquarters and make a missing person report. What kind of country is this, Smitty?"

"It's Oakland," I said.

"Smitty, I am concerned for Mei-ling. Are you sure she hasn't called you?"

"I'm sure." I answered. "I wouldn't worry about Mei-ling, Indy. She's capable of taking care of herself," I said, more to reassure myself than her.

"I do hope you're right. If she contacts you, please have her ring me up."

"Don't worry, Indy. You get some sleep and deal with the apartment in the morning."

"Thank you," she said, and hung up.

"Is everything all right, Smitty? Was that your friend?"

Dede was standing at the bedroom door in a white silk half slip.

"No, it was the woman she was staying with. Mei-ling's disappeared."

Dede must have heard the panic in my voice. She came over and stood behind me, and started to softly massage my shoulders and neck.

"It's going to be all right baby," she said.

Her voice was soothing.

"I ... I just don't know what to do, Dede."

She stepped over the couch and slid in next to me and gently gentle pulled me to her breast. "I know, baby ... I know."

I needed to get lost in her arms; to escape everything. I lifted my face and pressed my lips to hers. She didn't resist. Soon I was pressing against her as tightly as I could. She slowly stood up, took my hand and led me into the bedroom...

\*

The phone was ringing in the kitchen. I looked at the clock on the bed stand. It was one-thirty. Dede was fast asleep next to me. I eased out of the bed, made my way into the front room and grabbed the phone.

"Smitty? Is that you?"

It was Mei-ling. She sounded frightened and tired. She was at a liquor store down on MacArthur Boulevard. She was afraid to leave the store and they were getting ready to close. She had nowhere to go. I told her to hang tight; that I would be there to pick her up.

I slipped back into the bedroom and started to put on my pants when Dede rolled over.

"What's the matter, baby?" she said. Her voice was sexy in her semi awake state.

I quickly told her what had happened as I dressed, and that I was going to pick up Mei-ling and find her someplace safe to stay.

Dede sat up. "What do you mean; you'll find her someplace to stay? You'll bring that girl back here, Smitty. She'll be safe here. She can sleep in Chanel's room."

"Are you sure, honey?"

"You heard what I said."

I slipped into my shirt, socks and shoes and headed for the door.

"And Smitty. I'll make you a bed on the couch," I heard Dede's voice as I went out the door.

The section of MacArthur Boulevard that Mei-ling had ended up at lay alongside the 580 freeway; a stretch of cheap motels catering to prostitutes and drug addicts. Just a few blocks east were middle and upper middle class houses and apartment buildings that lined the well kept streets where I suspected her friend Indy lived. There were periodic calls to close down the motels that drew unsavory elements to the neighborhood, but despite an occasional slap on the hand, the motels thrived and the Indian immigrant owners and their patrons prevailed in holding on to their little piece of American free enterprise.

Mei-ling threw her arms around me and kissed me hard. I hadn't expected that kind of greeting, but I accepted it with pleasure.

She didn't ask when I told her I was staying with a woman friend, and I didn't offer any explanation.

I wasn't sure what Mei-ling thought when Dede greeted us at the door, but the fact that Dede was a beautiful young black woman didn't seem to faze her, and she accepted the hospitality graciously. I would have liked to think that she would be jealous, but like Dede, it didn't seem to bother her at all.

Dede took charge of Mei-ling as soon as we got in the door. She showed her the bathroom, and while Mi Ling was in there, Dede went to her bedroom and came back with a black silk night shirt. The toilet flushed and Mei-ling came back out. Dede took her into Chanel's room and closed the door.

There was nothing for me to do. Dede had made a bed on the couch for me, making it clear that I would be sleeping alone. I went to the kitchen table and poured myself some whiskey and lit up. I could hear the muffled sounds of the women talking through the bedroom door.

After Dede finally reappeared, she came over to me.

"She's a sweetheart, your Mei-ling." She laughed. She kissed me on the forehead and went to her bedroom.

After finishing my drink and my cigarette I undressed, turned out the lights and tried to get comfortable on the couch. I lay awake for some time unable to fall asleep; fantasies of making love to Dede and Mei-ling floated through my head until sleep overtook me at last....

\* \* \*

# CHAPTER 23

I woke to the sound of the coffee grinder. I had introduced Dede to Peets coffee when she and her grandmother were still drinking Hills Brothers. I instructed her on how much better it was when it was freshly ground. She fell in love with one of the African blends.

I lay on the couch half awake. It had been a restless night; I couldn't get settled and the thought of being in the same apartment with the two women in my life at the same time made me even more uncomfortable. But I was happy that Mei-ling was safe and that Dede was such a good sport about the whole thing.

"I'm sorry, baby. I didn't mean to wake you." Dede's voice floated over the top of the couch. "I'm heading for the UC law library to do some research and don't know how long I'll be. I put the coffee on for you and Mei-ling."

She came over to the couch and kissed me on the top of my

forehead like I was a child.

I waited until Dede left, then slipped off the couch and went to the kitchen table. The sun flowed through the window. I looked down on the lake. The morning joggers were making their rounds, playing king of the road with the thousands of Canadian geese that were visiting for the summer. I dumped the last cigarette from a crumpled pack of Luckys and lit up. The aroma of the coffee and the cigarette smoke was comforting.

"Good morning," the voice, sweet and familiar.

Mei-ling stood at the door of Chanel's bedroom. Dede's silk night shirt clung to her slim body. Her long black hair hung down over her shoulders and I remembered why I had fallen so fast and so hard.

"May I join you for coffee?" she asked shyly.

I couldn't take my eyes off of her. Words choked up in my throat.

"Isaac, are you alright?" she said walking into the kitchen.

I told her it was just that I was happy she was safe. I poured her a cup from the pot on the table, and I asked how she had ended up at a liquor store on MacArthur Boulevard at one o'clock in the morning in a neighborhood frequented by prostitutes and drug dealers.

She told me she had been staying with her friend from the university, which I already knew. When Indy went out to meet her boy friend, Mei-ling watched from the front window to be sure she got safely to her car. It was then that she saw the black Lincoln and knew who it was. She didn't have time to think of how they had found her. She grabbed her hand bag and snuck out through the back of the apartment building and started to walk until she found herself in the liquor store.

"I didn't want to get you involved, Isaac, but you persisted."

I smiled and took her hand. "It's a damn good thing I did," I said.

She squeezed my hand and smiled. "Your friend is a very nice woman."

"Let me explain about Dede and me," I said.

"It's okay, Isaac," she said. "She explained everything to me last night. You are lucky to have such a good friend."

She stared into the black liquid and the steam rolled up around her.

"I suppose I shouldn't be surprised they found me. You didn't seem to have any trouble."

She didn't say it, but I was sure she thought they had been following me since I left the marina, and for all I knew she was probably right. I was so panicked that I hadn't stopped to think.

I smashed out my cigarette and stared out the window. "Mei," I said turning back to her. "Why don't you just bail out on this whole thing? We could get on my boat today and head for Mexico."

She looked up from her coffee. "I told you before, I can't do that Isaac."

"Come on, Mei. Hell, it's just another smuggling gang. No matter what you do their will always be smuggling. And nothing will bring back your uncle," I said hopefully.

She bent her head down to the cup and sipped the hot coffee.

"I know that, Isaac. You don't understand."

"I'm trying, Mei," I said, hoping I didn't sound too desperate.

She was quiet for a moment, and then said softly under her breath. "Pandas..."

"What ... Pandas? What do you mean?"

"They are smuggling baby pandas out of China to sell to private collectors. Have you any idea how much they are worth, Isaac?"

"Baby pandas? So, they're smuggling baby pandas. So

128

what?" I said.

"Isaac, you just don't understand. Don't you see? If they can smuggle our national treasure out of China, and if the world knew of this ... well my government would appear incapable of securing its own borders. We would appear vulnerable and foolish in the eyes of the world. I can't let this happen, and I have vowed to do everything to stop it. This is what my uncle died for. Do you understand?"

"Pandas?"

I could tell she thought I was a dumb shit who couldn't see past the end of his pecker.

"I will do this or I well die trying," she said. "This is not your worry, Isaac, but now you're the only outsider to know this and you must not tell anyone."

I sat there. I thought about Johnny, laid up in the hospital because he had helped me; and of Peter, lying on the cold cement floor of the Hyatt Hotel as the life blood flowed out of him. It was my worry. I was ready to go down with her if necessary; not for the sake of her government, or even because I was in love with her, and certainly not for any fucking baby pandas. No, it was because of Johnny and Peter. It was because I had made a promise.

\* \* \*

# CHAPTER 24

Mei wanted to pick up the journal from my boat. We got to the marina and went to the gate when Skip intercepted us.

"Smitty, what are you doing here? We thought you took off last night."

"What the fuck are you talking about, Skip? Where's my boat?" I said.

"Well, if you don't know, someone must have hijacked it, because it wasn't here in the morning."

"The journal," Mei said under her breath.

"How could this happen! People don't just go around stealing 42 foot boats."

"You'd be surprised," Skip said. "Someone must have got in last night sometime."

130

"Shit, didn't anyone notice?"

"It's nobody's business when people come in or go out, Smitty."

"Well, shit. There must be something we can do."

I was getting desperate and Skip knew it.

"I'll report it to the Coast Guard. That's all we can do. If you're lucky they'll spot it before it gets into international waters. I'll make the call. Don't worry, Smitty. It'll be all right. That's what insurance is for."

We watched as Skip hurried back to the marina office, and then just stood there stunned. Insurance? Yeah, I had insurance all right. But they're going to be mighty suspicious since it had been less than three years since I made a claim on my Owens that had burned up under suspicious circumstances. Now this.

"The journal. They must have been after it," Mei said.

"Goddammit! My boat. It's all I have."

She took my arm. "You still have me, Isaac."

We walked back to my car and got in. I just sat there, not knowing what to do next."

"We have to find where they're keeping the pandas," Mei said. "My uncle had written something in the end of the journal. Just a note, but I think it was important."

I dug into my pocket and pulled out the page I had torn out. "This?" I said.

Before we started searching for Ridge Road I wanted to stop by the hospital to see how Johnny was doing. I filled Mei in on what had happened to him; that he was probably beaten up by the same thugs who were looking for her, and perhaps the same guys who had taken my boat. She wasn't surprised.

The nurse at the desk told us he was out of ICU and could receive visitors. Mei insisted we buy flowers.

*

"Smitty, you shouldn't have," Johnny said. He was surprised at this act of kindness until he saw Mei-ling standing behind me at the doorway.

"Mei-ling. I should have known Smitty wouldn't buy flowers unless he was forced to."

"How are you doing, Johnny?" Mei said. "Isaac told me what happened and why. I'm afraid it is my fault. I am very sorry."

"Seeing you here makes it all right, sweetheart. Smitty told me you were kidnapped. He didn't tell me he was the culprit."

We all laughed. It was a relief.

"I'm glad to see you're doing better, Johnny," I said. "I shouldn't have dragged you into this."

"Hey, I'm a big boy, Smitty. I knew what I was getting into. It could have been worse."

After the first greeting no one had anything to say; one of those uncomfortable moments when looking in on a sick friend at the hospital all eyes turn to the television for lack of anything better. Mei busied herself arranging the flowers in a plastic water pitcher. I just stood there looking at Johnny's battered face and feeling guilty. Johnny knew better than to ask any questions, or perhaps he just didn't want to know anything more then he already did. I wouldn't have blamed him for that. "Haven't watched TV during the day for I can't remember when," he said.

Just then a nurse came in. "You'll have to step outside for a minute folks."

"That's all right," I said, thankful for the reprieve. "We were just about to leave."

Mei kissed Johnny on the forehead.

"You get better soon."

"You're looking pretty good, Mei. Maybe I take you out dancing after I get out of here."

Mei laughed, and we headed for the door when Johnny

called me back. He motioned me to lean close to him.

"Smitty," he whispered. "The only reason I'm not dead is because someone scared off my attackers. I was only half conscience, but I heard a gunshot and someone shouting in Chinese. I don't know who it could have been, or if it means anything, but it seems you may have a guardian angel out there. I know I certainly did."

"Thanks Johnny. You just take it easy now."

I spotted them minutes after we started driving: the same black Lincoln: the same two hoods. They weren't making any secret about it, and all I could figure was they were trying to scare us off.

"We have to ditch the car," I said to Mei-ling who was sitting next to me with her hand on my thigh, as if we were high school sweethearts. At least that's what we did when I was in high school.

"Huh?" she said.

"We're being followed."

She looked back through the rear window and went for her purse. She was going for her gun. I stopped her

"No need for that, I have a plan."

I headed down to MLK Way and drove east toward Berkeley, checking in my rear view to see if the black Lincoln was still there. When we got to the Ashby BART station I pulled in and found a parking spot.

"We have to make this fast," I told Mei.

We jumped out of the car. A grabbed her hand and hurried to the station entrance just as the black Lincoln was pulling into the parking lot. We ran into the station, but instead of heading down the stairs to the train platform I led Mei through to the back entrance and pulled her around the corner and stopped. We stood there for a couple of minutes catching our breath. Then

I peeked around the corner, just enough to see the two hoods fumbling for money at the ticket machine. My plan worked. We waited to make sure they were leaving. Sure enough they walked through the turnstiles and disappeared down the escalator to the trains.

I took Mei's hand and we headed through the back parking lot and east one block to Shattuck Ave where an Enterprise Car Rental was located in what was once a gas station. All they had was a Honda Accord, nondescript and common in Berkeley and Oakland. Perfect.

I filled out the appropriate papers and handed the Enterprise guy my credit card, hoping I'd made my last payment and waved the customary inspection with a, "Don't worry about it. I'll trust you." I grabbed the keys and was out the door.


Ridge Road was an off shot from Tunnel Road which crosses over the Oakland hills above Highway 24 leading to the bedroom communities of Orinda and Lafayette.

I figured Peter's description "end" meant where the road ended. Turned out I was right. There were only a few residents along the road, and there was no sign of houses, only locked gates closing off dirt roads leading off into the stands off Eucalyptus and pine trees. Ridge Road end was no different. Locked gate. Barbed wire. Surveillance camera.

We stopped and got out of the car. The San Joaquin wind was picking up, blasting hot air onto the already parched underbrush. I could see why they called them the Diablo Winds. In Los Angeles we called them the Santa Anas.

It was fire season. But unlike the most people living in the hills I was fixated on Mei-ling and not worried about fires. She seemed especially sexy with a pensive look on her sculptured face. The wind wiped through her black hair. The only fire I was thinking about was in my pants and my urge to drag her into the brush and make passionate love to her.

"We have to go into the woods," she said, and I could tell it wasn't for the same reason I wanted to go. I knew nothing was going to stop Mei-ling. I was along for the ride.

\* \* \*

# CHAPTER 25

We walked off the road and down into the dry underbrush. The hot wind was whipping up the dust and roaring through the Eucalyptus and pine trees. The ground was blanketed with dry leaves and pine needles.

"There's got to be an opening in the fence somewhere," Mei insisted.

Suddenly the ground took a steep drop and we both fell and slid down on our asses clinging to one another. When we stopped she continued to hold on to me and for a moment I thought I might get lucky ... but no dice. Mei let loose and stood up, brushing herself off. She offered me her hand and helped me up. I must have twisted my ankle because it hurt like hell.

"Damn Mei, maybe we should turn back," I said. "They've probably spotted us in their camera."

"Don't be foolish, Isaac. Nobody sits and watches a surveillance camera. We've come this far, and I'm not going to let a fence stop me. Look," she said, pointing down the fence line. "There's a break up there."

It was against my better judgement, but love will do that to a man. She was a single minded woman, and determined to get in, and so we half slid down the slope and forced open the fence enough to climb through.

We made our way over a small hill. Mei pushed me to the ground and took her gun from her purse. At the bottom of the hill was a large ranch house with stables and a fenced in corral. The black Lincoln was parked in front along with two panel trucks.

"That must be where they're keeping the pandas," Mei whispered.

Then I heard a sharp voice behind us barking in Chinese. At least I assumed it was Chinese. But there was no mistaking the cold muzzle of a rifle pushing at the back of my head.

Mei turned her face to me. For the first time I saw fear there.

"Shit," I said

Then another bark from the man behind us.

"Get up, Isaac, or I think he'll shot us right here. She held her gun up to the man so he could take it.

"I told you this was a bad idea," I said.

We were marched down the side of the small hill toward the ranch house. I limped along the best I could. I could feel my ankle swelling up as our guard pushed me every time I slowed up.

A group of men came out from the ranch house and walked up to meet us. The hot wind swirled up little eddies of dust off the gravel road and roared through the trees. The men were all Asian, Chinese I figured, but what do I know? The exception was one white guy who, from his appearance, I guessed to be Russian. Probably a gangster; pure stereo type; short cropped hair, leather jacket, shades. The Asian hoods wore an assortment of tight tees or colorful Aloha shirts. They were all packing. They were all wearing Ray-Bans.

The man in the lead, a short stocky fellow with a bright colored shirt sporting a topless hula dancer walked directly up to Mei. A scar down his face made his dark angry expression all the more threatening. He spoke to her in Chinese and I could see her pretty face turn ugly with hatred. She lashed out at him only to be stopped cold by a blow to the face that sent her to her knees. My feeble attempt to intercede on her behalf got me a rifle butt in the gut, knocking the wind and machismo out of me, and I was on my knees next to Mei. A trickle of blood dripped from her mouth, but she was looking up at her tormentor defiantly. She shouted something in Chinese with such venom I couldn't believe it was the same woman. Whatever it was she said, it pissed the guy off more, earning her another blow that knocked her backwards into the dirt. All I could do was watch helplessly as the woman I was in love with was battered about like a rag doll. When the guy pulled out his pistol it was clear what he intended to do with it, but then the Russian guy grabbed his hand. He said something in Chinese and pointed to the horizon. A cloud of black smoke was rising from the hills behind us turning the bright day into a gray haze and the sun became a glowing orange ball.

The Chinese guy stuck his pistol back in his pants. He seemed agitated, but not by us, and for a second I was thanking a god I didn't believe in, because it was all I could do.

Two of the men picked us up off the ground as the others hurried off toward the barn.

The next thing I knew we were being tied to a post inside a small storage shed, and then the men left in a rush.

We were tied back to back. Neither of us spoke, expecting all the time to have the hoods come back to finish their work. Instead, we heard engines firing up, and a number of vehicles driving off, their tires crackling on the gravel road. It was then I noticed the acrid smell of burning brush and trees. The smoke was obviously a fire which was rapidly coming over the ridge by the direction of the dark cloud we had seen before being hustled off to the shed.

"They weren't going to shoot us, Isaac," Mei said quietly. "The Russian told them to let the fire get us, and to get the merchandise into trucks and out of here."

It was the fire the experts had been predicting, and it would be moving fast as the hot San Joaquin winds blasted it like a bellows on a camp fire. We knew about fire in California. Where most people in the country knew about hurricanes, tornados and blizzards, Californians knew about earthquakes, draught and summer fire. And the long hot dry summer had been plenty of warning this one was coming. The room was getting dark and I figured the fire storm was headed our way.

"Shit, they should have shot us. It least it would have been quick," I said, as if that was all I could say in the face of our impending death. I had always feared burning to death. Then I heard something from Mei that again surprised me about her. She began to cry, but it wasn't out of fear.

"I'm so sorry, Isaac. This shouldn't be happening to you. I should never have let you come with me."

It's funny the things you think when death is staring at you. I had faced death only three years before, but that was at the end of a gun, and I reacted in outrage despite being scared shitless. Hearing Mei cry like that made me just want to comfort her. But I couldn't think of any words so I just forced my hand back enough to touch hers.

"I love you, Mei-ling," slipped from my mouth, hoping that maybe the fire would bypass us. It happens.

Then we heard a car drive up and skid to a stop on the gravel road outside. Shit, they've decided to shoot us anyway.

The next thing I know the door swings open. I strain to see. It's the Ray-Ban guy. Rick.

"Holy shit," he said. "Just hold still and I'll cut you loose. We gotta blow this place like quick before we're all fried won tons."

I saw the switch blade snap open and slice through the rope

**139**

like butter.

By now my eyes were burning and my chest heaving from the smoke that was beginning to fill the shed. Thirty years of Lucky Strikes didn't help my screaming lungs.

"Jesus, I never thought I'd be glad to see you," I said, and began to cough uncontrollably.

He helped us out of the shed. We both supported Mei-ling who was still wobble, but insisting she was okay. I looked up; the fire was gobbling up the Eucalyptus trees along the ridge and coming down on us fast. Massive clouds of black smoke floated above the flames.

We squeezed into Rick's two seater Mazda RX7 sports job. Mei sat on my lap. Rick gunned the engine and we took off up the gravel drive way. The flames were all around us now, burning on both sides of the gravel road. We sped past the rented Honda which was engulfed in flames. Rick maneuvered around burning branches falling along the road. The heat was intense.

We finally hit Ridge Road and he took a quick turn east toward Orinda; a smart move because the easterly wind was blowing the fire west toward Oakland. Rick drove like a sports car driver along the winding road down into the valley. Sirens were blaring as a steady stream of fire trucks heading west into the hills.

Suddenly Mei-ling shouted in Chinese at the Ray-Ban guy. He shrugged his shoulders and held tight to the wheel.

"What the fuck did she say?"

"Your girlfriend is scolding me for not going after the smugglers instead of saving your asses," Rick said. "I have to tell you, Smitty, I was torn."

"You said that, Mei?" I asked, incredulous. She remained silent as her ass pushed against my lap, unconsciously grinding against me with every turn. If I said it wasn't getting my pecker hard I'd be lying.

"Well, I'm glad you decided to come get us," I said. "How the fuck did you know we were up here?"

140

"Your pal, Johnny. I wanted to check on him after the night before..."

"You're the one saved him?"

"Yeah. I'd been tailing you, and when he left your boat I decided to make sure he got home safe. I like Johnny. And his cousin makes the best pork bows in Chinatown. It's a damn good thing I did follow him. Anyway, he told me about the notation in the Major's journal, and I knew that's where Mei-ling would be headed."

Mei-ling refused to say anything, she just sat on my lap, moving around with every sharp turn as we raced down into Contra Costa County and away from the inferno; the best and only lap dance I ever had. It was funny; I realized then that Mei-ling and I might never be together again; that perhaps she was right, that we couldn't ever be together. And ironically our last sex was going to be just like our first encounter, only this time I wasn't sure she even knew or cared. That made me sad.

\* \* \*

# CHAPTER
# 26

Rick pulled into the Orinda House, the only bar and restaurant in the ritzy bedroom community. It had been a union house many years ago, but when a couple of toughs from the International Union showed up and tried to strong arm the owners, they got a taste of western justice; its been non-union ever since T h e parking lot was filled up, and it was no wonder from what we saw of the backed up freeway. According to the radio the fire had closed the Caldecott tunnel, blocking all traffic heading west into Oakland on Highway 24.

We got out of the car.

"I gotta make a phone call and take a leak," Rick said.

"We'll be in the bar," I said taking Mei-ling's hand. "I think we could both do with a drink."

Mei looked up at me for the first time and nodded in agreement. I wondered if she had even realized my reaction to her unintentional lap dance.

The interior of the Orinda house was like a museum of the west, with old black and white photographs of rodeo riders and past bartenders lining the walls. The place had an authentic look about it, not pretentious like some places where interior decorators try to make a place look authentic. Mei led us to the bar where we found two stools. Despite the crowd it was quiet with only the drone of the color TV perched in the corner which seemed to have everyone in a trance of disbelief as the Channel 2 news reports flashed aerial shots of the fire consuming homes in minutes as it went raging into the Oakland-Berkeley hills.

"What'll you have?" the bartender asked.

"A martini for the lady, and I'll have a double JD up."

"Make mine a double Stoli," Mei corrected.

"Some fire," the bartender said as he poured our drinks. "Been here twenty-five years and never seen the like. I knew something would happen when that damn Diablo wind started blowing."

I nodded and put a tenner on the bar and waved off change.

Mei took up her glass and downed the Stoli in one slug. "Another."

The bartender obliged. I downed my JD. It felt hot and comforting going down. My ankle still hurt, but the swelling had gone down.

"You?"

"Sure."

"This one's on the house," the bartender said.

Mei slid off the stool with her refilled glass.

"Let's sit at a booth."

I followed as she led me to a worn leather booth with a wooden table that bore the marks of lovers and motorcycle gangs.

"Give me a cigarette, Isaac."

I pulled a crumpled pack from my shirt pocket, dumped out two and lit them and handed her one. She took a long drag followed by a sip of Stoli and another drag, and then slowly exhaled the smoke. It seemed to relax her. For the first time I noticed the black and blue patch on her swollen cheek.

"Jesus, Mei, that asshole really smacked you hard. You okay?"

She touched her cheek and winced.

"It's all right."

"What about you. How's the leg?"

"It hurts, but I think it's just a sprain."

We sat there for a minute; her staring into her glass; me staring at her.

"So, what was that all about?' I finally said.

She looked up with a slight smile, like she knew exactly what I was saying but not acknowledging it.

"All what, Isaac?"

"That bullshit about your Ray-Ban buddy leaving us to become barbecue? Shit, the man saved our lives for Christ sake! I'm even starting to like the guy."

Mei looked back into her glass. I could see her mind was searching for what she thought might be the right answer, but there was no right answer.

"You just wouldn't understand, Isaac," she finally said, and took a sip of the Stoli.

"Try me," I said, taking a last drag from my Lucky and crushing it into the ashtray. .

She sighed. "We are from different worlds, Isaac. For a moment ... for a moment I thought maybe I could change, be like you. You made me feel that way, only..." her voice faded away.

Just then a collective moan came from the bar. I looked up at the TV. The fire was coming over the hill above the stately Claremont Hotel as Dennis Richmond, the anchor of Channel

2 News, announced that the fire was totally out of control. A spokesperson for the Oakland Fire department told Channel 2 News that they would make a stand to protect the historic building. The Claremont was 100 percent union. I had a lot of members there.

"You see, Isaac," Mei said, "this fire: you see it threatening that beautiful hotel that caters to the wealthy and makes jobs for your working class and you worry. In China it would be the People's hotel where those who work there could also vacation there. And because it belonged to the people, they would all come out and protect it. Here you have a fire department and a police department that are there to protect private property. The workers will not risk their lives to save the hotel. And, of course, the rich patrons would not. In China there is no private property. Do you understand, Isaac?"

I looked at her, and then glanced back at the TV. Mei sipped her drink and took another of my cigarettes.

"I knew you couldn't understand."

I lit her cigarette. She refused to lift her eyes to mine.

"I'm trying to, Mei-ling. Believe me, I'm trying. But what I can't understand is why you would give up your life, and mine, for some damned panda bears."

She took a drag from the Lucky.

"I was raised to believe that our personal lives were secondary to the good of the Revolution. I was a Young Communist and later in the People's Militia. It was my duty to protect our Revolution and China at all costs. My life meant nothing."

"But your uncle asked me to protect you?"

"Yes, Uncle Peter always felt responsible for me and he would protect my life if he could. But he gave his life gladly for China, and I can do no less."

Just then Rick came up to the booth and slid in next to Mei-ling. He laid a road map out on the table.

"I asked around and we can get back to Oakland through

the back hills. We just have to go around the fire.

He started tracing a route with his finger on the map for Mei-ling and they both slipped back into Chinese. It didn't matter because I wasn't listening. My mind was racing. Everything that had happened over the past few days; the intrigue, the danger, the passion, all deflated at once, leaving a void, as if my whole world had dropped out from beneath me and I was left drifting. Mei-ling's words had opened a chasm between us that I should have recognized long ago. I thought her feelings for me would close the cultural gaps, but I was wrong.

The words floated in my mind; you can take the boy out of the country but you can't take the country out of the boy, only this time it was the girl and China. Corny yes; but in this case, true. But it wasn't over, and I was still committed to my promise even if she didn't want my protection. I would see it through to the end.

"Excuse us, Smitty. I have to talk to Mei-ling for a minute," Rick said, as they slipped out of the booth.

I watched as they found a deserted corner. They seemed to be arguing about something, but even if I could hear them I wouldn't know what they were saying. Maybe if I could speak Chinese things would have gone differently between me and Meil Ling.

They returned and Rick told me it was time to head back to Oakland. I drank down the last of my Jack and slid out from the booth.

The ride back to Oakland was a circuitous one. We had to drive through the low lying hills, past the last existing farms and orchards that were slowly being swallowed up by ranch houses and shopping centers. Unfortunately, everyone else had decided to use the same route and the traffic was worse than on Game Day at Berkeley.

146

It took over an hour for us to hit the I-80 West at the sprawling town of Pinole and then south back into the Bay Area. Mei-ling had opted to squeeze into the small space behind the seats of the sports job. I could feel the distance between us. The only sound came from the smooth roar of the 194.0 cubic inch V-6 engine.

I tried to make conversation.

"This is one of my favorite sports cars," I said to Rick, and it was. I had priced them just for fun when they first came out the year before. "What happened to the RX 6?" I asked, remembering the Mazda I had seen him in across the street from Mei-ling's house.

'It's a lease," Rick muttered without taking his eyes off the road.

Mei-ling sat crouching forward with her arms draped over the two front seats. She stared at the road ahead.

No one was very talkative since we left the Orinda House. Something had happened, and I wished they would let me in on it. But it was obvious it was something they didn't want me to know about. It was aggravating.

Every now and again Mei said something to Rick in Chinese. Her voice was angry. He argued back, and so it went until we got back into Richmond, and then Berkeley. Traffic was still heavy and it was already dark. I could see the orange glow in the Berkeley Hills. The fire was still burning. How many houses were already lost to the flames? How many lives? Had the Claremont survived? It had only been two years since the Loma Prieta Earthquake, and now another devastating natural disaster. Oakland seemed cursed.

Mei-ling and Rick had been quiet for a while and I was thankful for that. We hit the interchange where the freeway split three ways; west to the Bay Bridge, south toward the Oakland Airport and, as I expected, Rick stayed in the left lane into north Oakland on Highway 580.

I took hold of Mei's hand that had been dangling over my right shoulder all the time.

"Can you drop us off at my apartment?"

"We're going to stop by Mei-ling's house first," he said.

I was worn out and I knew Mei must be too. All I wanted was a hot shower and a bed, preferable with Mei in it. But Rick was at the wheel and in control. I had to go along with the program, like it or not.

\* \* \*

# CHAPTER 27

If there is a god that watches over parking spots, Rick must have had an in because as soon as we drove up to the house a car pulled out right in front. We all got out and walked up the front steps, the ones I had first ascended in what seemed like an eternity ago. My ankle still hurt like hell, causing me to hobble along.\. I was wiped out, both physically and emotionally. At that point I didn't much care if Mei-ling came with me or not. She had been ready to sacrifice my life for her stupid pandas, and she had turned to ice since then. But I couldn't help my feelings for her. They were real.

We entered the still unlocked front door. Mei switched on the hall light and said something to Rick. But it was in Chinese again. He just nodded.

Nothing had changed since the last time I was there; drawers opened, pictures and papers strewn everywhere.

Rick said. "Let's go into the front room."

He let us lead the way. Mei switched on the overhead light,

and when I turned around to see what Rick was after, I saw the small automatic pistol in his hand.

"Hey, what the fuck's this?" I said.

"I am sorry, Smitty old buddy."

I looked at Mei, but she remained quiet.

I just stood there. It must be some sort of joke. Why would he want to kill me? Surely Mei would have said something if he was serious. But not a word as she moved out of the way. I looked into her face, but it revealed nothing. I told myself she couldn't be part of this, not after making love to me like she had.

"I'm sorry, but I got my orders, and orders are orders," Rick said calmly as he pointed the automatic at me.

Suddenly Mei stepped in-between us. "No, Huang!"

"We have our instructions. We can't take a chance on him spilling the beans; maybe to that reporter pal of his. He has to die Mei-ling. You know that."

I wasn't sure why he said it in English. Maybe he thought I'd force Mei to get out of the way to save her life. Or maybe he wanted me to know why he was going to shoot me in cold blood, and that maybe I'd forgive him. Either way, it didn't make much difference, or sense. So I just stood there, expecting the gun to go off any second.

Mei-ling stood her ground and shouted something in Chinese.

"Okay, you can die with him if that's the way you want it. Romantic; lovers die together in Chinatown," Rick said, as if he was writing a soap opera.

"Hold on there," I interrupted, "You can't just kill us and get away with it."

"Why not, nobody cares if a Chinese girl and her white lover are murdered here. This is Chinatown my friend. Nobody give a shit what happens in Chinatown."

"Well, if you have to kill me, at least leave Mei out of it," I insisted, not sure I was really prepared to accept my own demise. But it didn't look like there was any way out of this one.

Mei reached for my hand and I took it. "No Isaac. I won't let you die alone. This is all my fault."

At that moment it looked like the end for Smitty and his adventures into Chinatown when I heard the words I thought I would never welcome:

"FBI, drop the gun!"

It was Ted's buddy, Gabe Feinberg; gun drawn and identification open.

Rick looked startled. He slowly lowered his gun and turned around.

"Wait a minute, who the hell are you?"

"Special Agent Gabe Feinberg, and I'm telling you to put down the gun!"

Rick was indignant. "You can't touch me. I am Huang Xiabo, attaché to the People's Republic of China. I have Diplomatic Immunity."

"I know exactly who you are," Feinberg said. "You people may have been given authorization from my government to hunt down Chinese smugglers in this country, but we won't tolerate you killing American citizens. I suggest you go back to your car and hightail it back to your Consulate. Now drop the gun!"

Rick started to put his automatic back into his leather jacket, but Feinberg had other ideas.

"On the ground, I said."

"Wait a minute, you can't do that."

"I can and I am. You can pick it up at FBI headquarters in the morning. Now drop it."

I just stood there like an idiot as Rick carefully placed his revolver on the floor. I looked at Mei-ling and squeezed her hand. She was trembling.

"You haven't heard the last of this Agent Feinberg," Rick said as he started to walk out the door. "I will make a full report to my government." Then he stopped and turned around. "Smitty, I hope you don't hold this against me. You're an okay dude for a white guy. It was orders."

And with those parting words he left.

Mei-ling let loose of my hand and dropped down on the love seat we had shared on our first meeting.

"Isaac, give me a cigarette."

I dumped two out from my pack and fumbled around for my lighter, but when I tried to flick it my hand wouldn't stop shaking.

"Here, let me do that, Izzy," Feinberg said.

He took the lighter from my hand and lit our cigarettes. The first drag seemed to calm me. Mei-ling coughed.

"Everything all right in here, Gabe," a familiar voice came from the doorway.

"Come on in, Ted," Feinberg said.

"What's going on? I just saw some Chinese guy jump into a sports car and take off like he was in the Grand Prix at Monaco or something."

"Just a little misunderstanding," Feinberg said. "Seems the guy you saw is a Chinese agent who was about to turn your friends here into a crime statistic."

"For publication?"

Mei looked up at me. It was clear she didn't want me to say anything—spill the beans as Rick had put it—and I wasn't going to betray her trust.

But it was Feinberg who said, "Better not, Ted. This thing isn't over and that *shmuck* could be back looking for these two if it hits the papers. These people are very sensitive about having their dirty linen aired in public."

"Yeah, well my editor would probably nix it anyway, gutless prick. How about you Smitty, you okay?"

Friend or no friend, he would find a way to publish the story if he could. Ted wouldn't let anything stand between him and a good story.

I looked at Mei-ling who seemed to be relieved.

"Well, I ain't dead," I answered, "so I guess I'm doing better than I might have if Agent Feinberg here hadn't shown up. How'd you know where to find us?"

"You've been AWOL for a couple of days, so I called Gabe here, and we figured we'd keep an eye on Wu's house since it's the only place we could think you might go. What with the fire things have been pretty crazy around here. Gabe said he'd keep a watch."

"We're lucky he did," I said.

"Well, I gotta get out of here," Feinberg said. Gotta call coming in. from the wife and kids in the Catskills. Can't miss that. She'll think I'm fooling around on her," he laughed.

"Yeah, and if I don't file a story on the fire tonight my editor will shoot me," Ted added. "Can I drop you and Ms. Wu somewhere?"

"Can you give us a lift to the apartment," I asked, looking for an ashtray to douse my smoke.

Mei-ling picked one up off the floor and handed it to me.

"I think I'll stay here, Isaac. I should straighten up my house."

"I don't think that's a good idea, Mei." I said. "At least not alone."

"He's right, Miss. And I'd get some ice on that eye if I were you. Looks like someone gave you a wallop." Feinberg said, and made for the door with a "Shalom."

I hadn't really noticed before, but Mei-ling's eyes was swelling up.

"So, what it'll it be? You want a lift or no," Ted asked.

I looked at Mei.

"If you would like to stay, Isaac, I would like that."

"Okay then. You got any protection?" Ted asked.

"I have a gun upstairs," Mei said.

"And she can use it," I added.

"Well, okay then. But be careful. I'll check on you tomorrow."

He headed for the door and was gone, close behind Feinberg.

Mei-ling stood up and put her arms around me and pulled me tight to her. I didn't resist.

"I couldn't let him do it," she said.

I gently pushed her away so I could look into her eyes. They were red and tired and the bruise on her cheek was dark blue, but it just seemed to make her all the more attractive.

"You agreed to let him kill me?"

"Isaac, I was trained to obey orders, but when it was about to happen I couldn't do it," she said in a whisper. "I would have died with you." She hesitated for a moment. "I think I am in love with you."

I pulled her back to me and we kissed; a long kiss; a kiss that reassured us both we were still alive.


We showered together, running our hands over one another's body, scrubbing as if we could wash away the memory of the past day. Then we went to the kitchen and iced our wounds and sat there in nothing but our towels. Neither of us spoke. We just looked into one another's eyes.

After about fifteen minutes, Mei stood up and took my hand. She led me to her bedroom and we fell onto the bed. Mei immediately closed her eyes and was asleep. I lay there in the dark. She said she was in love with me. What did it mean for a Chinese Communist to be in love? Whatever it meant, it made me happy to hear her say it at last. I looked at her sleeping peacefully, the thin sheet outlining her naked body. I wanted to wake her and make love to her, but I was too exhausted. My mind wandered as the hot Diablo wind rattled the open windows and blew across my body. I was alive by some act of fate, and even though I didn't believe in such things, I didn't know what else to call it. Maybe in this case "karma"was the right word, or perhaps like the four rabbi's who defied God's will. It was the second time in less than two years I had barely survived a natural disaster, and the second time I had escaped being murdered. My life as a Business Agent at Culinary Local 4 had become a dangerous business. My leg throbbed, but I finally dropped off into a dreamless sleep

* * *

# CHAPTER 28

I opened my eyes and looked over at Mei-ling lying next to me. She had tossed off the sheets in the night. I kissed her lips and her eyes opened. She put her hand behind my neck and drew my face to hers. We made love; not the hot passionate, hungry love we had made before, but slow, sweet, generous love; the kind I had always heard long time lovers made. It was new for me.

We lay on our backs. The morning sun streamed through the window along with the slightly acrid smell of the fire. If not for the smell there would be no evidence that it had burned hundreds of homes, maybe even the stately Claremont. I could only guess how many lives were lost, but I did know of two that narrowly escaped, and the fact that it was Rick who had saved us, only to try and kill us a few hour later, only confused me more. They told me about Chinatown. But for now there were only the sounds of the nearby freeway and the morning Chinatown traffic. It was Monday, October 21, less than two years since the Loma Prieta Earthquake. I marked the date in my mind. But in

Oakland's Chinatown it was business as usual.

I got up and pulled on my shorts. The sun was streaming into the window.

"It looks like a nice day," I said. "We should celebrate?"

"Celebrate?" Mei asked.

I turned back to her. She had pulled the sheet back over her. I went back to the side of the bed.

"Sweetheart, you're free now. And we're alive. We should do something special."

She leaned up and kissed me. "I don't know what you mean, Isaac. I still have not found the pandas, and I am sworn to do so."

I pulled back. "Come on Mei. It's over. Your buddies at the Consulate want me dead and now they probably want you dead. You don't owe anyone anything."

"You still don't understand, Isaac. I owe my Uncle. I owe my country. I could never rest easy if I don't do this. Don't you see; we could never be happy together if I walk away now."

I sat down next to her. I should have known it wasn't over. I had jumped into something because of a promise to a dead man, and now I was sucked in totally by the love of a stubborn woman who I probably would never understand. I was way out of my league, just like everyone had warned me I would be.

She sat up, letting the sheet fall into her lap. Her black hair streamed over her breasts. She took hold of my hand,

"I don't expect you to come with me, sweet Isaac."

"But Mei, we don't have a clue as to where they might have gone, or even if they escaped the fire," I said, trying to reason with her when I knew there was no sense to it

"I know, Isaac, but one way or another I must keep looking."

"Well then, I suppose we should get started now." I said.

She smiled and put my hand on her breast. "We don't have to start just yet, Isaac."

The burly waiter dropped the plate of cha shu pork, fried eggs and steaming rice in front of me. Mei was munching on a Pork Bow, probably baked in Johnny Wong's cousin's little bakery the night before. It was a hole in the wall Hawaiian/Chinese café squeezed between the huge Green Jade restaurant and the Bank of Canton. Mei said it had been Peter's favorite place to get breakfast before reporting for his morning shift at the Hyatt.

"There must have been something Peter said or did that was out of the ordinary; something that might give us a lead," I said.

Mei took a sip from her coffee mug. It was one of those heavy brown mugs that were popular in diners in the forties and fifties, and for a moment I felt like I had been transported back in time; like I had become lost in a black and white noir movie.

"It wasn't strange that he was acting differently that last year," Mei finally said, pulling me back to the present. "But he tried his best to keep everything from me. I know he was trying to protect me."

I attacked the sweet cha shu, smearing it into the egg yolk, and shoveled it into my mouth.

"There must have been something?" I repeated.

She took a bite from the cha shu bow. "I love these," she said, and washed it down with coffee. "There was one thing I remember. But I don't think it meant anything."

"Well?" I said, scooping a chop stick full of the sticky rice into my mouth and following it with hot coffee.

"One day a couple of weeks before he..." she hesitated. "Before he was murdered he had come home late. I was studying when he came in. He said he wanted to take a tour of the wine country. I thought it was odd because my Uncle was never particularly interested in wine outside of what he served at work. He wanted me to go with him and that we could make a day of it."

"Well, that's not so strange," I said. "He was probably under a lot of pressure. I mean, going undercover like he was. Probably just wanted to relax and spend some time with his lovely niece."

"Yes, you are probably right, Isaac." She went back to devouring the pork bow. Then she looked up. "But there was something. I didn't give it much thought at the time, but for some reason he wanted to go by a small winery in Glen Ellen. Most of the big wineries are in Napa, and this seemed kind of out of the way. But he insisted. Oh, never mind, it was probably nothing.

"Go on," I said. 'It could be something."

"Well, we found the place. It was isolated way back in the hills. We just drove past. It didn't have a tasting room and it seemed deserted. There was a For Sale sign in front. I didn't think about it at the time. I guess he read about the place somewhere and was curious."

I thought about it for a while as I finished my breakfast. The waiter filled our coffee cups, dropped a check on the table and went back into the small kitchen without saying anything. I could have sworn I'd seen him in Hawaii Five-O.

"I think we should look into it," I said.

Mei looked up. She was pouring sugar into the coffee. "What? Why, Isaac?"

"Because, it's all we got." I reached across the table and took her hand. "Besides, I know a neat little bed and breakfast in Sonoma. It would do us both good to get out of here for a couple of days. Do you remember the name of the winery?"

She thought for a moment. "Not really, but I think I can find it."

"Finish your coffee and let's get out of here."

I sent Mei-ling back to the house to pack some things to take with us. But, I needed a car. The union car was at the BART station where I had left it ... at least I hoped it was still there. It may have been towed away.

*

I walked to the Union Hall where Marta gave me her usual surly greeting, and buzzed me into the inner office. Gil was sitting at his desk in the President's office.

"What are you doing here, Smitty? You ready to come back to work? It's been hell around here since the fire."

"No brother, but I got a problem."

"Sit down my man. Talk to me."

"Well, I had to leave the car at the BART station on Ashby, and then with the fire and all, I couldn't get back to it. I'm afraid it got towed."

"And you need some wheels, am I right?"

"As rain."

"Don't sweat it, Smitty. I want you to take my car. It's out back. I have the other union car and I won't need mine. Besides, I got three more cars at home."

"Shit, Gil, you don't have to do that. I could take the union car."

"No, I'd rather you take mine. I'll check and see if your car's been towed. Don't worry about it."

He tossed me the keys.

"It's out back. Have a good time."

Gil was a big hearted guy, but I didn't realize how generous he was 'til I went out to the rear parking lot and saw his car— a bright cherry red Chevy Camaro convertible.

* * *

# CHAPTER 29

We were on the pass leading down into the Napa Valley from the Vallejo Fair Grounds and past Marine World on Highway 12. Mei had been thrilled when I drove up to her house in the Camaro. She wanted to drive, but I reminded her that she didn't know how to drive.

The rolling hills of Napa, which only a few years before would have been filled with dead stalks of corn, brown in the late summer heat, were now green with row upon row of grape vines. Ever since California wines began to rival those of France and Italy, and wine making became the hobby of the rich and famous, huge mansions had sprung up everywhere, with adjoining ultra modern wine making facilities and visitors lodges, all surrounded by thousands of acres of premium agricultural land where one crop reigned..

We stayed on Highway 12 heading west toward Sonoma, along a winding two lane road that took us through small communities with businesses that looked like they had been there for years. We were in Sonoma County, and while there were vineyards here, they weren't as dominate. Most of the farms and small businesses along the highway reMeined the same as they had always been, with small patches of corn fields, corrals with a couple of horses or cows, or a small poultry farm with flocks of white turkeys running around getting fat for the Thanksgiving slaughter. The houses all needed paint, and some were barely standing. And so it went for about twenty miles until we drove into the town of Sonoma.

I headed for the town square. It was a typical Spanish style plaza with restaurants and shops surrounding the city park on four sides. The plaza itself had the traditional fountain where little kids cooled off in the summer, and a band shell for weekly concerts. City hall sat right in the middle.

I found a parking place and asked Mei-ling if she was hungry. There was an old fashioned soda fountain that served sandwiches. But most importantly there was a pay phone and a bathroom. I needed to make a couple of calls, the most urgent being to the bed and breakfast joint to see if we could get a room for the night. It was a week day and past Labor Day so I thought my chances might be good.

There wasn't any room at the soda fountain's counter, so we found a small table by the window looking out over the plaza. While Mei was looking over the menu, I hit the head and made my calls. Luckily there was a vacancy at the B&B, a last minute cancellation. Next, I called Ted at his office. He was in.

"Where the hell you been?" were the first words out of his mouth. Not, *how are you?* or *I've been worried about you*, but: "Didn't you learn anything after last night?" he scolded.

I told him where we were. "I thought after all we had been through, it would do us good to get out of town," I said, trying to sound casual.

"Well, Gabe called to see how you were doing and I felt like a fool because I didn't know where the hell you were. Something's going on and you're not telling me, your best friend who saved your ass last night."

"I'm sorry, Ted. This thing is really complicated."

"Smitty old comrade, why the hell can't you just find some

nice normal woman and settle down? Every broad you've gotten mixed up with the last few years gets you involved in some kind of shit, and you always seem to nearly get yourself murdered. I don't know how many times I've told you not to get involved in Chinatown. Why don't you listen to me?"

I didn't like being balled out, especially since he was right, but I wasn't about to admit it.

"Give me a break, Ted. Don't worry about me. I'll keep in touch."

"You do that."

He hung up. I knew what Ted was really pissed off about; he sniffed an important story behind all this. He was concerned about me, yes, but he was also a reporter, and I knew that breaking a major story about Chinese smugglers and U.S. Government complicity with Red China was more than any reporter could pass up. I felt guilty for keeping him in the dark. But I promised Mei I wouldn't tell anyone, and I intended to keep to my word.

I returned to the table.

"I ordered hamburgers and milk shakes. I hope that's okay with you."

"Perfect," I said, pulling the old fashioned metal chair back and dropping into it. "What flavor milk shake?"

"Vanilla. I hope you like it."

"Perfect."

We had been carrying on small talk since leaving the Bay Area; that is, when we talked at all. There had been long moments of silence. I chalked it up to Mei coming down from everything that had happened over the past week, and hoped it was because she just felt comfortable just being with me. I still couldn't read her; she reMeined a mystery, despite her admitting she was in love with me. But the question that nagged at me reMeined; what did being in love mean to a Chinese Communist, even one who'd spent the past decade in America?"

We ate our hamburgers and washed them down with the

milk shakes. The place was as good as I had remembered it from the last time I had been there; the shakes where thick and the burgers plump and juicy. Mei seemed to like them. She finished before me. I leaned forward and wiped the milk shake from her upper lip. For a moment I thought she was going to kiss me. But no, she whispered secretively;

"That man over there. I think he's following us."

"Huh?"

"He' came in while you were on the phone. It was like he recognized me or something," Mei said. "He's sitting at the counter with a Giants base ball cap on."

"Chinese?"

"No Isaac, he's Caucasian ... like you."

She kissed me briefly and then leaned back in her chair.

"Pay the check and let's get out of here."


We came out of the soda fountain. I glanced back as we crossed the street to the plaza but I didn't see the guy. He was either a professional, or Mei-ling had been mistaken. But when I spotted him waiting by the fountain as we made our way through the plaza I was convinced. Only what I didn't know was who he was or why he was following us.

We got in the car. "Did you see him, Isaac?"

Yeah. He's tailing us alright." I started the car and drove out into the traffic.

By the time we arrived at the Sonoma B&B I had identified our tail's car; a light beige Ford sedan. As I pulled into the gravel driveway, the car zoomed past and disappeared down the road.

The Sonoma B&B was a large restored three story farm house with a porch running entirely around the outside overlooking an acre of beautifully tended flower gardens and fruit trees. Off to one side was a chicken coop, and nearby a large vegetable garden where an old Mexican man was hoeing. The place was

164

owned by a friendly middle aged couple from back east. The wife welcomed us and showed us to our room on the second floor. She told us we were lucky; they were booked solid for the whole month. The wine country was booming.

"Breakfast is at nine. I hope you have a nice evening."

The room was furnished with turn of the century antiques, including the large canopied bed covered by a thick flowery quilt. There was a complimentary bottle of wine on the table with two crystal glasses. Mei fell back on the bed and put her arms out to me.

"This is wonderful, Isaac."

I took her hands and willingly let her pull me gently on top of her.

"No matter what happens tomorrow, tonight let's pretend we are a young couple on our honeymoon."

We kissed, lingering with our lips pressed together for a long time...

We both dozed off. When we woke it was dusk and I suggested we go for dinner. There was a decent Italian place near the plaza.

The young waiter sat us near the wine bar and gave us the menus. It was a nice place, what you'd expect in the up and coming tourist trap with tens of thousands of people coming from all over the world for wine tasting at the countless wineries. Prices were moderate but with antipasti, salad, entrée, and wine you could easily blow a hundred bucks.

Mei looked over the menu. "You suppose we can get a cocktail before we eat?"

I was surprised the waiter hadn't ask, but hey, it was non-union like I said, and waiter turnover was probably high. I flagged the maître d'.

"Can we get drinks before we order?"

"Of course, didn't your waiter ask?"

"He must of overlooked it," I said, not wanting to get the poor fellow in trouble. "Oh, and can we smoke?"

"I'm sorry sir, but I can get you a table in the patio. It's quite nice."

"That will be fine," I said.

We followed the maître d' into a small outdoor patio with linen covered tables surrounding a small fountain. It was a warm evening, and the smell from the hanging wisteria that decorated the place was refreshing. So we sat down, and I pulled out a Lucky, offering one to Mei. She declined and I lit up. Too much natural beauty made me uncomfortable. A waiter came over and we ordered drinks, Jack Daniels and a vodka martini. Then I saw Mei's eyes widen.

"What is it? I asked.

"Him," she said. "He just came into the restaurant."

She was facing the glass patio doors and could see the interior of the restaurant. I had to look around. There was no one.

"You sure."

"Yes, Isaac."

"That's it," I said. "I'm going to see who this joker is."

"Isaac," she grabbed my hand. "Don't make a scene."

"Don't worry, Mei," I said and got up.

It wasn't hard to spot him. The restaurant wasn't very busy. He was the only one sitting at the wine bar. He was wearing a subtle Hawaiian shirt, slacks and white tennis shoes; in his fortes with bushy black hair and a twelve o'clock shadow, he could have been anyone. I went up to him and tapped him on the shoulder.

"Can I help you?" he said in response.

"Who the fuck are you, and why are you following us?" I

said, getting right to the point. I surprised myself for being so bold, but with everything that had already happed I didn't give a shit anymore.

"I beg your pardon. Have I seen you somewhere before?"

"You know damn well you have."

"I'm afraid you must be mixing me up with someone else, pal."

He turned back to the bar and called the bartender over. "Let me see your wine list." Then back to me. "Look pal, I'm just a wine buyer, up here looking for some good product." He produced a business card from his pocket and handed it to me. I glanced at it:

Herman P. Goodfellow
Buyer – International Wine Exports
San Francisco, CA

I handed him back the card.

"Keep it," he said. "Now, if you don't mind, I have to get back to business."


"He's lying, Isaac" Mei-ling said. "You saw him. He is the same man who was at the place we ate this afternoon. And I am sure if we check, he's driving the same car that was following us."

Our drinks were already on the table. I took a sip of the bourbon.

"The wine buyer thing must be a front," I said. "But why is he following us, and who is he? If he was Chinese, or even Russian, I would be sure we're on to something up here. But this guy? I don't know."

"I'm not hungry, Isaac. Let's finish our drinks and go back to the...what was it's called?"

"Bed and Breakfast." I said.

"Bed and breakfast. Yes. Let me have one of your cigarettes."

I asked for the check and told the waiter we wouldn't be eating after all. I was sorry. I had my eye on the Sopa de Pesci with fresh Dungeness crab.

* * *

# CHAPTER 30

We drove silently back to the B&B. The gravel road to the house was pitch-black. I parked and we got out. A warm breeze was blowing. The air was fresh with a clean smell you never get in the city. It was a moonless night. I looked up at the sky. It was filled with stars and I could see the Milky Way like a cloud of light sweeping across the sky. It's odd how we forget these things when we live where the lights of the city swallow up the natural night sky.

"It's beautiful," Mei said. "Let's stay out here for a while."

We stood there with our arms around each other and just looked up into the stars. The only sounds were the lonely croaking of frogs.

We went up to our room. I opened the wine and we clinked glasses. It was a decent Merlot. Then we undressed in silence, turned out the light and made quiet love.

Mei immediately fell asleep. I just lay there in the darkness. My mind raced. The quiet was unsettling. I had always lived in one city or another, growing up in New York and LA, and then San Francisco and Oakland. Without the drone of a faraway freeway, or the traffic on the streets and occasional siren, I was out of my element. Besides, I was hungry. I finally dozed off around two o'clock.

We made our way downstairs in the morning. There were three other couples already sitting around the large dining table. A spread of fresh croissants, breakfast pastries, toast, bagels, scrambled eggs, bacon and fresh fruit were on the side board. I took a bagel, scramble eggs, bacon and coffee. Mei filled her plate with fresh fruit and wheat toast.

There was a German couple who apparently didn't speak English, or just didn't want to talk to Americans. An elderly couple was chatting with the third couple who were middle aged tourists from the Midwest. They welcomed us with "Good Mornings." The other couple seemed uncomfortable, as if they had never seen a mixed race couple, even in this day and age. Something's never change and I wondered what they would have thought if I had been with Dede.

Mei, noticing their reaction and deliberately kissed me. The older couple asked if we were on our honeymoon. Mei blushed. It had been like a honeymoon, but I knew the party would be over as soon as we walked out the door of the Sonoma Bed and Breakfast. It would be back to business. If I told anyone we were on a quest to find a bunch of panda bears smuggled out of China, they would have thought I was a mad man and I would have to agree.

Highway 12 between Sonoma and Glen Ellen is not the most

scenic; running past small businesses that lined the side of the road catering to the needs of people living in the country. The gas stations were the same as they had been thirty years ago. We passed through Boyes Hot Springs which at one time had been a major getaway for people from San Francisco with its health resorts and hot mineral baths. Lately it had fallen on hard times and seemed stuck in the good old days that weren't so good any longer.

We took a left onto a small road that led down into the small town of Glen Ellen, past the entrance to the Jack London Historic State Park where fans of the author of "White Fang" and "Call of the Wild" could walk down a long path to what reMeined of London's dream house in the woods. The Wolf House, as he called it, mysteriously burned to the ground before it was completed, taking with it London's wealth and health.

Ever since leaving Sonoma I had checked in the rear view mirror for the beige ford to see if we were being followed, but no sign of it. Mr. Goodfellow, or whatever his real name was, could have easily changed cars before picking up our departure from the B&B in the morning, and followed us unnoticed. The red Camaro was not hard to spot. On the other hand, I could just be feeding into Mei's overly cautious paranoia, and her phantom stalker was just that, a phantom.

I pulled into a dirt parking lot in front of the Glenn Ellen Country Store and parked. The day was heating up and it promised to be a scorcher. It was funny, but ever since we left the Bay Area no one had mentioned the fire, a major disaster in their back yard.

"Well, this is Glen Ellen," I said to Mei. "You got any idea where we're going?"

Mei looked around. "It's been a while, Isaac. Let me think for a minute."

"I'll go inside and get us some cold drinks. Anything you like?"

"Ice tea."

I stepped out into the bright sunshine and went into the store. I could feel the sweat dripping from my forehead. It was a bit cooler inside, but not much. It was a typical country store with everything from groceries to poultry feed to farm implements. The bank of refrigerators in the rear of the store had a full array of cold drinks. I got Mei an Arizona Ice Tea and grabbed a bottle of Anchor Steam beer for myself.

The old man at the counter smiled.

"Where you from?" he asked innocently.

"You ask everyone comes in here where they're from?"

"Well friend, I know all the locals, and I make it a hobby to ask where folks are from. Get all kinds coming to see London's place."

"Sorry pal, the heat's got me a little on edge. We're from Oakland."

"Oakland. Quite a fire you folks had down there. radio says it was real bad. Killed a bunch of folks, they said."

"Yeah, it was pretty bad, but let me ask you something."

"Shoot," the old man said."

"You're the first one I've met since I've been up here to even mention the fire. Why's that?"

The old man shrugged. "Superstitious. Folks figure they talk about it, it might happen here. Been a mighty dry summer."

"Strange," I commented. "How much I owe you?"

"Buck-fifty. You folks on your way up to Stover's Ranch?"

I pulled out my wallet and handed him two dollars. "Why do you say that?" I asked.

"Well, I couldn't help notice your girlfriend in the car is Asian. Pretty girl from what I can see." He opened his cash register and dropped the two bills in and came out with a fifty cent piece. "Anyway, a car full of Asians came in late yesterday evening in a black Lincoln. They had a panel truck behind them. They got a bunch of beer and left. Not very friendly. But the

172

one white guy—Russian fellow I think, judging from the accent —asked how to get to Stover's Winery. So, I thought you and your gal might be on your way up there."

"Didn't it strike you as odd all those Chinese men coming through town?" I asked

"Not particularly. We get a lot of Japanese tourists coming through to see the State Park, but this weren't no tour bus. Old man Stover passed on a couple of years ago and the place been vacant. Word is it been sold recently. Maybe these guys are setting up some kind of Buddhist temple or something; seen lots of that sort of thing around here over the past twenty years. An ashram, I believe they call it. Don't know what the Chinese call it. Indians—Native Americans—used to think this Valley was sacred and that seems to draw a lot of religious nuts. On the other hand, these guys didn't look like the religious type, but what do I know. Anyway, I thought maybe that's where you two might be heading."

"Stover's Winery?"

"Yeah, you know the way?"

"I'd be grateful if you told me," I said.

It was a stroke of luck, or maybe not so lucky. At any rate, the old man gave me directions. I thanked him and walked back out into the sun, debating whether I should tell Mei what I found out, or just let it go and maybe she'd give up and we could go home. Foolish. I knew I'd tell her.

\* \* \*

# CHAPTER 31

We continued on Arnold Drive which served as the Mein street of the small town and crossed back over the Sonoma Highway to Trinity Drive as the old man had instructed. It was a winding road that took us up into the hills on the north side of what was known as the Valley of the Moon. It was slow going and seemed forever until we hit Wall Road where I made a left into the wilderness. There were no visible signs of houses, only an occasional Meilbox in front of a gravel road that disappeared into the brush and scrub pine. It was afternoon and the sun was beating down on the car. The air conditioning in the union car never worked, but it rarely got hot enough in Oakland to be necessary. The Camaro was another story. Gil took care of his

174

cars and the Camaro was just one in his collection. But Mei had nixed it, and told me to put the top down. I pulled over and fidgeted with the instrument panel until I found the right button. Now the sun beat down on us mercilessly. But Mei loved it, laying her head back on the seat with her eyes closed, allowing the sun to beat down on her face while the wind wiped through her hair.

"You and your uncle came all the way out here?" I asked her. We hadn't spoken much since we left the market. She nursed her ice tea and shrugged. I think she was pissed that I had found out where we were going when she couldn't remember.

"He said he wanted to see this winery," she finally said. "Don't ask me why. As it turned out there was nothing to see and there was nothing around that would make someone think it was a winery. The gates were locked. We're going in the right direction. I remember now."

"Well, it's a good thing the guy at the market knew where we were headed. We could have been driving around these hills forever."

Mei just looked out at the passing stands of Oak, pine and eucalyptus trees and huge black berry patches.

I spotted a Meil box with a sign:

Stover's Winery.
No Trespassing. No Hunting.

"Not very friendly," I said, as I pulled onto the gravel road. We followed it for about a quarter of a mile when Mei told me to stop.

"The gate is up around the next bend. Let's get out and take a look."

"Why not just drive up?" I asked.

She shot me a look like I was some kind of dumb shit. I hated that, so I shut up. We got out of the car and took to the side of the road, making our way through the brush. I let Mei take the lead and was thankful we didn't run into any of the massive wild black berry bushes that were all along the road.

When we got around the bend Mei ducked down. I followed her lead hiding in the dry bushes. My body was soaked with sweat. Invisible bees seemed to be swarming all around us by the sound of their loud buzzing. We could see the gated entrance. The black Lincoln was parked behind the gate and a man was standing guard.

"Shit Mei."

"What is it, Isaac?"

"Don't you recognize him? It's the same fucking sonofabitch that caught us at the last place."

"You swear too much, Isaac."

"Don't you recognize him?

"Of course I do. I'm not blind."

I looked at her. Cool as a cucumber; no sweat on her face.

"I think we ought to get the hell out of here," I whispered.

Mei continued looking at the entrance. Then she turned to me.

"For once I agree with you. Maybe we can get a place to stay in Glen Ellen, and plan how we're going to get in there tomorrow."

It wasn't what I wanted to hear, but it would give me time to talk her out of it. I took her hand and we made our way back to the car. I knew all the talking in the world wouldn't change her mind, but I had to try.

I had noticed a vacancy sign at the Jack London Lodge when we drove into Glen Ellen. Luckily, it was still up when we got back around five in the afternoon. It had been a long hot day and all I

176

wanted was a cool shower and a drink. I parked and looked over at Mei-ling. She looked like a sexy wild woman with her hair blown into a tangle. She had unbuttoned her blouse and tied it in front of her so that it wrapped around her small breasts and exposed her round belly and slightly crooked belly button. She reached behind her to pull her hair back into a ponytail, jutting out her breasts in an alluring pose that made me want to jump on her right there, heat or no heat. But I knew there would be no honeymoon night at the Jack London Inn. Mei was in her duty to Uncle and Country mode.

We checked in. The receptionist remarked on how lucky we were to get a room without a reservation, and apologized because the air conditioning in the room was not working: "Burned out last night. Repair man is supposed to be here soon, but who knows."

"It's been our lucky day," I said, wondering if the lack of air conditioning had anything to do with the room being available.

When we opened the door to the room it was like an oven. Mei threw open the windows and we both started to strip with the same idea; so it would be a shared shower, something I was sure Mia hadn't counted on because there was no way we could be naked together and not make love and she knew it.


I lay on the bed as the hot air blew over my wet body through the open window while I admired Mei standing naked in front of the large mirror on the bathroom door with a towel wrapped around her head like a turban. Then I heard the entrance door start to open and jumped up. Mei hurried back into the bathroom and shut the door. I grabbed the door and held it just before whoever was on the outside could get it opened.

"This room is occupied," I said.

"Oh," I heard from the other side. "I'm here to fix the air

conditioner. Didn't know anyone was here."

'Well, there is. Give us a few minutes and we'll let you in and get out of your way."

"Sure thing, friend. Sorry about that."

When I turned around Mei had already slipped into some clean tight jeans and a baggy Cal T-shirt. She had packed some things before we left Oakland. I, on the other hand, was stuck with the same clothes I had been wearing for the past couple of days. They were soaked in sweat and smelled it.

"Let's see if we can't find somewhere to get a drink and some food," she said.

I hurried and got into my dusty denim pants and wrinkled, sweat stained white shirt.

"I wonder if there's some place to buy some clothes."

I opened the door. The repair guy was waiting patiently. "It's all yours," I said.

"Should take about an hour or so," he said as he picked up his tool box and stepped into the room, looking at Mei.

She smiled.

"Is there some place in town we can buy some hiking equipment?" she asked.

"And some clothes," I added.

"Well, there's a used clothes store down the street that should be open," he said, watching Mei as she stepped toward the doorway. "As for hiking gear, you'll have to go into Sonoma or Santa Rosa."

I followed Mei out the door ignoring the repair guy's approving wink.

We didn't have to go far to find a bar and restaurant. The "Saloon" inside the hotel had a full dinner menu from the adjoining restaurant, appropriately called the Wolf Room. I told Mei I'd feel better getting some clean clothes first, but she insisted we have a drink and a cigarette before we went anywhere.

"Don't worry about your clothes," she said. "We're in the

country."

I didn't blame her, after all we'd been through over the past two days, and nothing surprised me about her anymore. The more I learned about Mei-ling Wu the more attracted I was to her. The demure lady in the sexy green dress with the dragon embroidery I had first met was a woman of many dimensions.

We slid onto the bar stools and ordered our usual; vodka rocks for her, straight Jack Daniels for me. The Bartender gave me the once over, like this pretty Chinese gal had dragged some bum in off the street. We took our drinks to a table and I lit two Luckys and handed one to Mei. She took a long drag and exhaled the blue smoke in a steady stream.

"Do you think it's a good idea to go back," I ventured. "I really don't want to go through the same experience we had the last time we saw these guys."

She took a sip of the cold vodka. "Isaac, you know I have to go. And I know you will come with me, so can we not talk about it anymore. I need to think."

She took a longer drink and took another drag from the cigarette. Then she abruptly stood up and announced she had to make a phone call.

I watched her cute little ass sway as she walked away. "What the fuck," I mumbled to myself and took a slug from of JD. Then I noticed the man walking toward me...Herman Goodfellow, the guy who wasn't following us. He walked right up to the table.

"We must be on the same tour. I've found some fairly good vintages. You?"

I looked up at him. "Have you tried Stover's winery?" I asked, hoping to catch him in a lie.

"Stover's? Never heard of it. Any good?"

"Stinks," I said, and took a drag from my cigarette.

"Thanks friend. I'll skip it. You know, cigarettes ruin your taste buds. "

"Thanks, I'll keep that in mind." I took another drag and

smashed the Lucky out in the ashtray.

"Well, I have to find a place to stay. This joint's booked up. Nice seeing you."

"Right."

Mei came back to the table and finished her drink without sitting down.

"Let's go find you some clothes. Those really stink,"

"Thanks."

* * *

# CHAPTER 32

Anne's used cloths store was a small shop across the street from the Glen Ellen Country Store. The sun was starting to drop behind the hills as our entrance was announced by a little bell over the front door. The shop was crammed from floor to ceiling with clothing. Three rows of neatly pressed dresses, blouses, shirts and pants on hangers left little room between them. Antique dresses hung from the walls. The place had a faint smell of patchouli.

A woman appeared from a back room. She wore a full length granny dress, but she wasn't anybody's granny. Her long brown hair was tied back in a braid that reached her ass. She looked to be in her thirties and had a wholesome beauty even with the lack of makeup. Long dangly earrings hung down to her shoulders.

"Hi. My name is Heather. Can I help you?" she said in a

warm greeting.

Mei smiled at her. "My friend here needs some clean clothes."

The woman looked us over with an approving smile.

"I can see that," she said. "Seems the heat has gotten to you. There's is a laundry in town."

"This is all I have," I said.

"Take off that shirt," Heather ordered.

I suddenly felt self-conscious, and looked at Mei.

"Take it off, Isaac."

Both women helped me strip the sweat stained shirt. Heather took my grimy T-shirt and tossed into a garbage can. I felt pampered and liked it. The woman took the shirt and looked it over.

"Nothing a good wash and iron won't straighten out.

"We haven't got time," Mei said. "Can we buy something?

"That's what I'm in business for, but I won't feel comfortable taking your shirt. I'll give you credit depending on what you choose.

"That's very kind," I said, standing there half naked with my arms folded across my hairless chest.

"Well, let's see what I can find. I have a great selection of authentic Hawaiian shirts," Heather said proudly as she started fidgeting around the racks.

Mei joined her.

"Just a plain white shirt will do," I said.

"Nonsense," the woman said. "Here's just the thing."

She pulled out a bright blue shirt with a hula dancer and palm trees painted on it. "Just the thing to go wine tasting."

"Too bright," Mei said. "Try this one, Isaac."

She produced a black cotton shirt with a subtle tropical design.

"And some pants," she added.

"I have a good selection of jeans if you like. Or a pair of

Dickies or Big Bens if you prefer."

"That would be great," I said. "Union made."

"Well, I don't know about all that. Let me see, thirty-six long and...thirty-six waist?

"Thirty-four" I corrected.

She pulled a pair of khaki color pants from the rack and handed them to me.

"You can try them on in the back. Just leave your old pants on the floor. I'll credit you for those too."

We made our way back to the Inn. The light material of the shirt felt good against my skin as a warm breeze stirred the evening air. Mei remarked how good I looked in the shirt. I felt like a tourist. All I was missing was a Nikkon slung over my shoulder. I smiled at her.

Over dinner and a drink in the Saloon I told Mei about Goodfellow.

"Claims he's not following us, but I find that hard to believe."

Mei just shrugged as she dug into her Club Sandwich.

"We'd better get some more suitable cloths when we go into Santa Rosa in the morning", she said as she chewed.

I wanted to know what she was planning, but instead just started eating my hamburger. I was probably better off not knowing.

After we finished we had a cigarette and sipped our drinks.

"I asked that woman, Heather, if she knew anything about the Stover Winery while you were changing," Mei said.

"And?"

"Well, first she started to laugh. She said the old man changed the name from 'Stover's Ranch' to 'Stover's Winery' a couple of years before he died. He told everyone that since every other place in the Valley had turned into a winery he may as well just change his place's name and fit in. I didn't know what was so funny."

I couldn't help but laugh. "Don't you see the humor in that," I laughed.

"Why, because he was conforming to what the majority where doing?" she said sincerely.

I laughed again and kissed her on the cheek. She accepted the kiss with a straight face.

"I never did understand your Americans humor."

"Never mind," I said. "Did she mention anything about our friends up there now?"

"She confirmed what that old guy at the market told you. Seems everyone assumes any Asians moving up here have to be some kind of Buddhist sect. They seem to forget that Chinese workers and farmers have a history here as long as white people do."

"Well, if these guys are Buddhist, I'm a Mormon," I said.

"I thought you were Jewish, Isaac."


I could hear a hum from outside the door. We went in and a blast of freezing air hit us.

"I guess he fixed the air conditioner alright," I said and hurried to adjust it as Mei opened the window to let the warm air rush in.

There was no lovemaking that night. I was dead tired and crawled into the bed. Mei sat staring out the open window smoking another cigarette. I turned the TV on and switched to the 10 o'clock news to see if there were any reports on the fire. Turned out that was all the news on the report. The fire killed 25 people and injured 150 others. It burned an estimated 1,520 acres, destroyed 3,354 single-family dwellings and 437 apartment and condominium units. The economic loss was estimated at $1.5 billion. My eyes grew heavy. Mei wasn't paying any attention. She must have still been planning our next move. The last thing that went through my mind before dozing off was how I hoped it wouldn't turn out like the last time.

Mei shook me awake as the sun streamed into the room through the open drapes. "Come on, Isaac. I want to get an early start."

"Where are we going?" I asked, as she hustled me out of the room.

"Santa Rosa. There's a Sears Department Store there. We can get appropriate clothing and a few other items we'll need. And I want to stop by the county records department."

It was too early to question why we needed special things, or what she had planned for us. But the opportunity to buy some new underwear and socks was enough motivation for me. Why she wanted to stop at the county records department ... well I stopped trying to second guess Mei a long time ago.

"We should keep the room," I said. "I'll want to take a shower before we go anywhere."

"Don't worry, Isaac. I already informed the desk we'd be spending another night."

\* \* \*

# CHAPTER 33

Highway 24 into Santa Rosa is a straight shot between the hills that make up the Valley of the Moon. The sun was starting to beat down on the Camaro, but I knew Mei would object to putting up the top and turning on the air conditioning. What good was having a new car with all the luxuries if you didn't use them? The road was dotted with small turkey farms, antiquated gas stations and small businesses in-between wooden houses in various stages of decay. As the hills started to recede we hit the road going to Calistoga with its mineral water spas and health resorts. Another mile and small tracts of new suburban ranch houses started to spring up along the highway as we entered the

Santa Rosa city limits.

I pulled into a gas station, not one of the old fashioned ones we had passed earlier, but a modern Chevron station with a mini mart. The damn Camaro gulped down gasoline like a Tenderloin drunk guzzles cheap wine. I wondered if my car had been ticketed or towed for overstaying its welcome at the BART station. It wasn't fancy, but at least it wasn't a gas guzzler. I went in to pay for the fuel and asked the attendant how to get to the Sears store while Mei went to the bathroom.

Ten minutes and another gallon of gas later we drove into downtown Santa Rosa and found the Sears. It was an older store; the modern day shopping malls hadn't caught up to Santa Rosa yet and it still had an old town feel to it.

I let Mei take the lead; first the woman's sports clothes section where she bought camo shorts and a safari shirt. Nextshe led me to the man's sports cloths section where she insisted I try on some camo pants. I declined. The ones I had bought at Anne's used cloths would be fine. I settled on a shirt similar to the one she had bought. It was as if we were going on a safari or some such foolishness, but I kept my mouth shut. Next we were fitted with hiking boots. I picked up a three pack of Fruit of the Loom boxers and T-shirts, along with a package of sweat socks; all I really had wanted.

To my surprise Mei pulled out a wad of bills from her bag and paid for everything. I didn't ask about that either. The next stop was the sports department where Mei selected a powerful flashlight, some wire cutters, a small back pack and a gallon can of Coleman fuel. Now it was as if we were going on a commando raid or something. When she stopped at the gun counter I tried to put an end to it.

Still, she insisted, but was told by the man behind the counter she couldn't purchase a gun unless she was a U.S. citizen. She turned to me and I just shrugged. The gun salesman informed us it would take three days for a back ground check before he could sell us anything. I was grateful.

Next stop; the Sonoma County Administration Center. I had no idea what Mei wanted there, but she obviously knew exactly what she was looking for. She marched me to the Office of Records on the third floor where a middle aged man stood behind a long counter. He looked like he had been there his whole life; a seasoned bureaucrat.

"What can I do for you?" he asked in a not very friendly tone.

Mei gave him a big smile, the first I has seen from her since our escape from the fire. It seemed like years ago.

"We're from U.C Berkeley," she said flipping out her wallet with her faculty identification so the man could see it. "We're doing archeological research on the Native Americans in the Valley of the Moon and need to see a typographical map of the area off of Trinity Road in the vicinity of Wall Drive. Any assistance you can give us would be of great help," she said in her sweetest voice.

It was another facet of Mei-ling I had never seen before. I stood there feeling foolish. It was getting to be a too familiar feeling.

The stone faced bureaucrat's face melted into a smile.

"I think I can help you Miss Wu. In fact," he said proudly, "we have aerial photographs of that area if that would be helpful."

"That would be extremely helpful."

"Just give me a minute while I fetch them for you," he said, and scurried off to a bank of enormous drawers; the kind architects use for plans and diagrams only multiplied a hundred fold and reaching to ceiling.

"How the hell you know all this?" I whispered.

Mei looked at me with a straight face. "I did archeological research back in China," she said matter-of-factly.

The man returned with several large sheets which he laid out for us to look at.

"Yes, here it is, don't you agree Isaac."

I looked, pretending like I knew what she was talking about, and nodded my head.

"Can we get a blow up of this area here? I believe it's a place called Stover's Ranch, or Winery. That's where we will be looking."

"Certainly," the man said. "It will just take a few minutes."

"I can't tell you how helpful you have been," Mei said. "Let me have your card so we can be sure and give you credit as a resource in our paper."

His face lit up like a Christmas tree. "That would be wonderful," he said and hurried off into a back room with the large photograph.

It was a hot ride back to Glen Ellen with the afternoon sun beating down on the canvas top of the Camaro. Mei had let me put it up, but she refused to turn on the AC. We didn't talk; Mei studied the photo copies, remarking only that it was helpful that it was marked with longitude and latitude. I had no idea why that mattered; we knew where we were going, but I preferred to not think about it.

Back at the Jack London Inn I headed straight for the Saloon. Mei said she'd join me shortly and to order her a tall vodka on the rocks.

The bartender greeted me with, "I see you found some clean cloths."

I was in no mood for jokes. "Just pour the drinks."

I was starting on my second JD and Lucky when Mei came and sat next to me. She had changed into the camo shorts. The bartender and the other man at the bar stared at her as if they'd never seen a woman in shorts before.

"How do I look?" she asked unexpectedly.

"You look really sexy in those shorts," I said.

"This is what we wore when we were in the Jungles of Vietnam on special assignments." She smiled.

Women like to be flattered, even Chinese Communist women apparently. I could see why the Russian "advisor" had taken a special interest in her.

"We'd better get something to eat and then take a nap. We'll be starting out after dark," she said.

I wasn't particularly hungry but figured I'd better eat something. It might be my last meal. Then I heard a voice from down the bar.

"Who let the gook whore in?"

I turned toward the man sitting at the end of the bar. He had made his remark to the bartender, just loud enough so we could hear.

"You got a fucking problem, mister?" I said.

"Yeah, I got a problem," he answered.

"Well, fuck you," I said as I slid off my seat and was ready for anything.

Mei grabbed my arm.

"Forget it, Isaac."

"Fuck that," I said.

The bartender reached across the bar and took hold of the man's shoulder.

"That's enough, Mike. You get your ass out of here and go home or I'll call the cops."

The man the bartender called Mike hesitated. He stood up and headed for the exit.

"Fuck this..." were his parting words.

The bartender came over as I sat back down.

"I'm sorry about that. Mike's a vet. He ain't been right since he came back from Nam."

"Come on, Isaac. Finish your drink and let's get something to eat."

"I'm not hungry." I said. My hands were shaking.

*

Back in the room Mei turned to me. "Isaac, make love to me." She put her arms around my neck and pressed her body against me. Then she kissed me hard and passionately. And that's how it went; passionate, urgent love, like the time when we first lay on the floor of her house after the gun shot that had nearly killed her. Only this time, we tore each other's clothes off and clung to one another so hard that sweat soaked our hot naked bodies as we pounded and twisted against each other. The last thing I remember before falling into a deep sleep was Mei whispering in my ear:

"I love you."

*　*　*

# CHAPTER 34

The next thing I knew Mei was gentle shaking me awake.

"It's time we get going, Isaac.

I glanced at the clock on the bed side. It was one-thirty in the morning

"It's the middle of the fucking night. Can't we just make love again and go back to sleep?" I said hopefully, knowing it was a waste of time.

The Saloon was closed down with a gate in front of the entrance. Outside was completely quiet save for the constant croaking of frogs. It was a week night and the little town had shut down. I supposed things livened up on the weekends. But for now it was like a ghost town. It was a clear night and once again I was amazed at how many stars there were. A warm breeze blew in from the East; all in all completely alien to this city boy.

We climbed into the Camaro. Mei threw her back pack into the back seat and we took off down Arnold Drive past the Glen Ellen Market and Anne's Used Cloths store, on up to the highway and across to Trinity Road, retracing our route from the day before. Mei had become all business, as if the passion of the night before had been channeled into the mission ahead of us.

The road was pitch-black without a light in sight. I drove slowly along the curving road as we climbed into the hills, braking several times for a deer or some other animal scampering across our path. All my concentration was focused on the headlights ahead of me, lighting up the cracked pavement as my world shrank down to that narrow confined area. Nothing else existed. There was no room to think about what lay ahead.

"Slow down," Mei said. "We should be coming to Wall Road soon."

After about five minutes we came to a road on the left. I couldn't make out the street sign, so I stopped the car and got out. I reached up to the sign and flicked my lighter: Wall Road.

"This is it," I said, as I got back into the car. "It's still not too late to turn back."

She gave me one of those looks I had become all too familiar with.

"Shut off the headlights," she said.

"What are you talking about?" I said. "I can't possible drive down this road in total darkness. We'll end up in a ditch."

"Just wait a few minutes, Isaac. It will be okay."

I didn't know what we were waiting for. I just sat there next to the woman I loved on a warm summer night, parked on a dark country road, and there we sat doing nothing. I thought, if only it were under different circumstances it would have been a perfect romantic night.

"What the fuck are we waiting for Mei?"

"Just a couple of minutes, Isaac. Be patient."

Then suddenly a full moon started to appear over the hill, slowly at first, and then rising into the black sky casting an eerie blue light over the entire valley, and I understood why the Indians believed it was a sacred place. I looked up the road. It glowed in the moon light.

"Okay, we can go now."

I put the Camaro into drive and started slowly up the road.

I had to ask. "How the hell did you know that was going to happen?"

"I read the local newspaper in the hotel, Isaac."

I had no come back to that, so I just kept driving until Mei told me to stop. I had no idea how she knew where we were, but she seemed sure of herself.

"Alright Isaac. We walk from here on. If I read the aerial photo right we should be able to work our way around to a spot behind the ranch. We'll have to be very quiet."

She pulled her back pack from the back seat, covered the interior light and opened the door. Then I saw the pistol she took from her purse and dropped it into the back pack.

"What's that for," I asked.

"Just come on if you're coming," was her curt reply.

I got out and quietly shut the door. There was no turning back now.

I followed Mei into the brush. I stumbled forward until we hit a barbed wire fence. I was glad I had long pants on and wondered if Mei was getting scratched up in her sexy camo shorts. I was already out of breath and promised myself for the millionth time to stop smoking. The other side of the fence was cleared pasture. Silhouettes of the ranch house and several out buildings surrounded by oak tress glowed in the spooky blue moon light. I llooked back were the Lincoln was stationed in front of the front gate.

"No guard," I whispered. "Maybe he saw us coming."

"Don't be silly, Isaac. He's probably asleep in the car. Come on."

We moved along the fence line crouching low so we were partially hidden by the brush and tangles of blackberry bushes that shed long shadows over us. My back was aching and I was breathing heavily out of my mouth so it dried up like a desert. The breeze had stopped and I was sweating like a pig.

Suddenly two bright lights appeared, coming up on the inside of the fence. Mei grabbed me by the hand and pulled me back into the bushes. I was thankful they weren't thorny blackberry. She urged me to lie down on my stomach alongside her. Her breathing was heavy, but she lay perfectly still with her arm over me protectively as if I were a child. I felt grateful just for the physical contact and obvious concern she had for me. I should have been scared shitless, but instead I felt happy having her next to me, and I knew I would do anything for her.

The two lights belonged to a jeep with two men in it. It drove on past. We waited as the red tail lights faded into the darkness.

"Okay," Mei said. "We can go now."

I rose and followed her back to the fence and we continued in the direction the jeep had come from.

It seemed like hours, but was probably more like ten minutes.

"Mei, wait a second," I whispered. "I have to stop."

"What's the matter, Isaac?" She said looking back at me.

"I have to rest my back for a minute, and catch my breath."

Her lips curled up into a smile. "Why Isaac, you never complained about your back when I made love to you."

"Okay, let's keep going," I said, resigned to keep moving and totally humiliated

"Good," she said, and we moved on.

After about ten minutes we stopped. The back of the ranch was about two hundred yards away. A light burned in the back window. Mei dug into her back pack and came out with the wire cutters. As she skillfully began clipping away at the barbed wire I caught my breath and wiped the sweat from my face. She cut a neat hole, just big enough to crawl through.

"Okay Isaac, let's go."

I took a deep breath and started to follow her through the hole until I felt a burning pain in my leg. I looked back and saw that I had gotten caught in the barbed wire.

"Shit Mei, I'm stuck."

She looked back and crawled next to me. I felt her hands manipulating my leg to get it unstuck from the fence. Finally I was able to pull my leg through the barbed wire and I was okay except for the pain. Mei pushed my pant leg up.

"It's only a scratch," she said. "You'll live."

"Yeah, for now," I said.

We stood up and started walking toward the ranch. Crouching would have done no good since there weren't any bushes, and I don't think even Mei was willing to crawl all the way.

We were about half way to the closest out building when we both froze as the headlights appeared in the distance. Then Mei dropped to the ground as a search light flashed in our direction from the jeep. I reMeined frozen for a second, like a deer caught in oncoming headlights. Mei reached up and pulled me down, but I was sure they had spotted me.

I was right. The headlights turned away from the fence line and started heading in our direction. Mei jumped up.

"Come on, Isaac." She whispered loudly.

"I got to my feet and we started running toward the closest building. I looked over my shoulder and saw the headlights getting closer and then I tripped, falling flat on the hard ground.

Mei stopped to help me, but it was too late. The jeep screeched to a stop, kicking up a cloud of dust, and the two men

196

jumped out with automatic rifles, shouting in Chinese.

"God damn it," I said, holding onto Mei as the men stopped in front of us. One of the men pushed us to our knees while the other shouted something in Chinese. Mei put her hands on her head.

Déjà vu, we were fucked, and I didn't believe a rescue was in the cards this time. I had to do something, so I lunged toward the man who had pushed us down and grabbed hold of his rifle when I felt a blow to the back of my head and I hit hard ground flat on my face. After that everything was a blur. I could hear Mei scream something in Chinese and then saw one of the men stuffing a gag into her mouth while he held her head back by her hair. I made a feeble attempt to rescue her but was greeted by another thump to the back of my head and everything went black.

\* \* \*

# CHAPTER 35

The next thing I knew, I came to and my head was throbbing. I was in total darkness, but I could feel my hands touching someone else. It took me a moment to realize I was tied back to back with Mei. I could sense her; recognize her smell, the sweet odor which gave off a hint of gardenia flowers. Our hands were bound together and our legs were tied. We must have been in one of the out-buildings.

Then I heard, "Are you alright, Isaac?" and my assumption that my prison mate was Mei was confirmed.

"Aside from the hammer inside my head, yeah," I answered.

"That was foolish of you, Isaac."

"You're right."

We sat there, back to back, in silence for a while. I was afraid Mei blamed me for getting us caught, but there was nothing I could do about it now. My eyes began to adjust to the dark and I could faintly make out my surroundings, but there was nothing much to see; an empty storeroom.

"I wonder why they didn't take us to the ranch house, or just shoot us on the spot?" I said.

"They said they would wait until morning and let the big boss decide what to do with us. That's what they said, anyway," Mei answered curtly. There was sadness in her voice, masked by her anger.

"Mei, are you alright? Are you mad at me?"

"No Isaac. It's just that I have failed to avenge my uncle, and I have failed to carry out my mission."

"Yeah," I said. "Well, I guess I failed too."

"How did you fail, Isaac; by following me?"

"I failed to keep you safe as I promised your uncle I would, and now we are probably both going to die."

She didn't respond, so I let her be. We sat in the dark, waiting. There seemed no way out. I started to think about dying, and for some reason it didn't seem to matter. I had no family and few friends. I had spent my days fighting for ungrateful union members who were always too busy to attend union meetings or walk a picket line. What difference had I made on this earth; what difference if I were dead. The only thing I cared about was Mei-ling."

Then I felt the warmth of Mei's body next to me and I shook the self-pity, moribund thoughts off and started pulling at the ropes.

"What are you doing, Isaac?" Mei said, breaking her silence.

"I'm trying to get fucking loose, that's what I'm doing. We owe it to your uncle to at least try. God damn it, Mei, we owe it to ourselves. We can't just give up."

She was quiet for a moment and then started to move her hands around against mine.

"I can feel the ropes loosening, Isaac. Just concentrate and pull back on the ropes. It will be easier for me to work my hands free. They're smaller than yours."

I could feel the sweat dripping from my forehead. My hands were hot and wet with sweat as the ropes burned into my skin until suddenly the pressure let up, and I could feel her hands slip away from me, and the pressure on my wrists was released.

"I'm free," Mei said.

I relaxed for a moment as the blood flowed back into my hands and my shoulders started to work again. Then I easily slipped the ropes from my wrists and I was free.

Mei moved around to me and undid the ropes from my ankles. I slowly stood up. My legs were cramped and hurt, but I got to my feet. Then Mei reached up to me and I pulled her into my arms. We clung to each other for a moment, as if reassuring ourselves we were alive and free from our bonds. Then she slipped from my arms and knelt down as if searching for something.

"My back pack," she said. "They just threw it down on the ground somewhere."

She was going on about finding where they kept the pandas, and how we had to complete the mission when I heard a distinct noise ... a rapid thumping sound that seemed to be growing closer. I had seen enough war flicks to recognize the sound. It had to be a helicopter — a large one, hovering above us.

Mei found her back pack and pulled the pistol from it. Then she became aware of the sound.

"A helicopter?' she said.

Then there was a sharp snap from where the door was and it started to open. The beam from a flash light pierced the darkness and the shapes of two people appeared in the blue moonlight that flowed in through the door.

"Shit, they're flying the pandas out and they've come to finish us off," I said.

"Not without a fight," Mei said, checking her gun.

Then I heard a familiar voice.

"Izzy...Miss Wu."

It was Gabriel Feinberg, Ted's FBI buddy.

"Mei put down the gun. They're on our side. Over here," I said as the flashlight beam shined in our faces.

The two men approached us.

"Who are you?" Mei asked accusingly.

"Gabriel Feinberg, FBI. And this is my partner..."

"Robert Berman, your friendly wine buyer."

"Goddamn, two Jewish FBI agents," I said, and then I laughed, sending my head into a fit of agonizing pain. It seemed like an eternity. "I knew you weren't no fucking wine salesman," I said.

Berman laughed, but he was cut off by his partner.

"We got to get out of here."

By then the sound of the helicopter had grown deafening, and we could see powerful spotlights flashing outside. Then the sound of automatic rifle fire crackled in the darkness and grew in intensity until it sounded like an all-out war was going on.

"Come on," Feinberg said. "Before we all get caught in a cross fire."

"What the fuck's going on? Who's in the helicopter?" I said.

"Ask your girl friend," Berman said, grabbing me by the arm.

Feinberg pulled Mei up. I looked at her, but she looked away. That's when I knew what those mysterious phone calls back at the hotel were all about.

We hurried outside the storage building. I looked over to where the ranch house was. There were flashes of gun fire coming from inside the building, but it was no match for the heavy weapons the camouflaged men from the helicopter were shattering the place with. We ran up the road leading to the front gate where a plain gray Ford sedan was parked alongside the familiar Lincoln Towncar. A body lay sprawled out on the ground next to it. I figured it was the guard. My legs were heavy from fatigue and just raw fear. Again I glanced back. The ranch house and all the out buildings were now engulfed in flames, including the one we had just been in. If the two FBI guys hadn't shown up and pulled us out of there we would have been incinerated, just as I figured the men in the ranch house, and assumable Mei's precious Pandas.

Mei stopped and turned. She reached out for my hand and held it tightly. I could see a faint smile cross her lips as the flames from the fires danced in her eyes. A tear rolled down her cheek...

* * *

# CHAPTER 36

The gray Ford took off down the gravel road with the two FBI agents in the front seat and Mei and me in the back. We sped past the red Camaro which I had parked off the side of the road.

"Hey, aren't we going to stop so I can get my car?"

"Sorry pal," Berman said turning back to face me. "You'll have to worry about that tomorrow."

"But it's not mine," I insisted.

"Sorry pal."

"Don't worry about it, Isaac," Mei said taking hold of my hand and tucking it between her warm bare thighs. "It will all work out."

I hadn't thought about the bashing my head took in all the excitement, but now it started throbbing with pain again.

` "What the fuck was that about?" Feinberg said to anyone in general.

"I don't know," berman said. "And I don;t think I want to know."

"You fellas have an aspirin?" I said.

Feinberg took one hand off the wheel and reached into his pocket and produced a small brown vial. "Vicodan. Works wonders."

"Water?"

Berman passed back a half empty bottle of Calistoga. Mei took it dumped out two tablets.

"Here, Isaac."

Without thinking I popped the tablets into my mouth and swallowed them down with a gulp of water. Mei took my hand again and but it back between the comfort of her thighs. I lay my head back on the car seat and tried to relax, just as the car bumped off the gravel road onto Wall Drive. I shut my eyes and tried to sleep, but my mind was moving a thousand miles a minute: Had Mei known the helicopter would arrive? And, if she did why had we gone back there? It didn't add up. But she surely reported to someone about the whereabouts of the smugglers. Questions that I knew I might never get answered, because I would never ask.

I was suddenly cold. My eyes opened and I saw San Pablo Bay off to the right. The temperature must have dropped twenty degrees. I had been asleep for nearly an hour. Mei was curled up on the seat with her head in my lap. Her breathing was slow and steady, but she must have been freezing in her shorts.

"Feeling better, Izzy," Feinberg said.

I could see his face in the rear view mirror.

"I'll live," I said. My head was a bit fuzzy and then I remembered I had dropped two vicodans.

"Good. We'll have you safe and sound at your apartment on Lakeshore in about half an hour," Feinberg said.

"How the fuck do you know where I live?" I said accusingly.

"Come on Izzy, we're the FBI. We know everything."

Berman laughed. "Your buddy the reporter told him."

"Figures."

Mei stirred and lifted her head. "Where are we? It's awfully cold."

Berman produced a blanket and handed it back.

"We keep it for other purposes," he said. "But it should keep you warm. Sorry, the heater doesn't work. No money in the budget to fix it."

I spread the blanket over Mei and she dozed off, nestling her head in my lap again, surprisingly stirring my passion, or was it the vicodan?

No one spoke for the rest of the way. Feinberg merged into the left lane of the freeway as we passed through Richmond, El Cerrito and Berkeley which took us to Highway 580 South at the interchange near the Bay Bridge. He got off at Grand Avenue as Mei started to wake up.

"Where are we, Isaac?"

"We're almost home," I said.

Mei sat up and pulled the blanket up to her neck. She rested her head on my shoulder and put her hand on my leg. We passed by the east end of Lake Merritt and made a right onto Lakeshore. This time I didn't plan on sleeping on the couch. Dede would understand.

Feinberg drove slowly along the Lake until we came to the apartment building on the left. He pulled over on the lake side curb.

"Okay Izzy, you're free to go."

"What about Mei," I said, bewildered. "Isn't she coming?"

"Sorry pal," Berman said. "Ms. Wu has to come with us."

"What do you mean? She's here legally." I protested.

"Our orders are to bring her in," Feinberg said. "I'm sorry Izzy. That's the way it is,"

"Mei?" I said.

She put her finger to my lips. "It's okay, Isaac. It has to be this way."

Then she kissed me. It was a hard passionate kiss; a kiss that seemed to say goodbye. Then she pushed me away.

"Go home, Isaac. You have fulfilled your promise."

I couldn't figure out what was going on. I was in a daze as I stepped out of the car into the dark Oakland night and watched as the gray Ford pulled away and drove off down Lakeshore until its tail lights disappeared from view. I looked out onto the Lake. The necklace of lights sparkled through the early morning fog that had settled over the city. It was a typical cold Bay Area Autumn night. For the first time I noticed that there wasn't a living sole in sight. The street was deserted. It must have been four o'clock in the morning. A feeling of total loneliness swept over me. I should have protested more. I should have made them let Mei come with me. But I didn't, and now there was nothing left for me but to walk across the empty street to the apartment.

I saw the kitchen light in the apartment. The other window was dark. I started to climb the stairs leading to the entrance. Dede would be there. She would reassure me, and tell me everything would be all right. She would go with me to the Federal Building in the morning and we would find Mei.

I unlocked the security gate and walked through the darkness to the apartment door, and knocked softly and rang the bell. Dede was a light sleeper. She would hear me. But no one came. Finally I put my key into the lock and carefully turned it so as not to make any noise. I slipped into the open door and closed it behind me. The apartment was deathly quiet. I made my way down the narrow hallway to the living room/kitchen area. The light on the kitchen table was on and a note pad rested on the coffee pot. I sat down at the table and looked out the window at the lake. The sky was turning gray with the coming day. I took the note pad and read:

*Dear Smitty,*
*I don't know if you will read this because I haven't the slightest fucking idea where the fuck you went with your girl friend. But if you do get home I've been called back to Arkansas because my aunt has fallen ill again. I hope everything is alright with you and Mei-ling. She is a beautiful woman – too good for the likes of you. The little I know of her from our talk the other night she seems like a very sweet and intelligent person, and I hope everything works out for the two of you. If you need me for anything you can call*
*Your devoted friend always,*
*Dede.*

She left a phone number with an Arkansas area code. I went to the cupboard and took down the bottle of bourbon I kept there and brought it back to the table with a glass. I lit up a Lucky and stared out the window as night slowly became day.

\* \* \*

# CHAPTER 37

I woke up on the couch with a blanket over me, although I couldn't remember how I got there. Sunshine was flooding the room. I got up and stumbled to the kitchen table where the empty bottle of bourbon and crumpled pack of Luckys still sat next to Dede's message. The digital clock on the coffee maker said it was twelve-thirty.

I went to the cupboard to see if there was any coffee. No luck. Dede had cleaned the place thoroughly before she left, and that must have meant throwing a lot of stuff out. But I needed coffee and some food before I could do anything. I took a hot shower, and then headed out the door for the Merritt Coffee shop.

On the walk along the lake my head began to clear. There were a lot of things I had to do: Call Agent Feinberg; tell Gil his car was left abandoned in Glen Ellen, and if my car was still at the BART parking lot, hoping the BART cops had been too busy with the fire to go around ticketing cars over staying their welcome. But first things first. I stopped at the liquor store next to the Merritt and bought a *Tribune* and a pack of Luckys. Then I went into the coffee shop. The smells from the attached bakery mingled with the aromas of cooking. Everything seemed so normal compared to the past couple of nights. It all seemed like a dream now; a good dream or a bad dream? There was Mei, and the night at the Sonomo B&B when we made love like a newly wed couple. Then there was the Stover ranch, the blow to my head - that still hurt - the dark store room and the ropes; the rescue and then the helicopter attack like something out of a Rambo flick; and finally losing Mei in the darkness of the early morning. It all seemed unreal as I slid onto the seat at the counter like I had done so many times before, and the waitress poured me a cup of coffee and took my order. The Merritt hadn't been the same since my friend Flo retired. I would have to pay my own bill.

"Eggs, scrambled, sausage and rye toast. Make sure they toast it dark."

I watched the line cooks for a minute as they worked their magic at the grill, like a ballet of culinary skill. Then I opened the paper to see if there was any mention of the battle in the hills above Glen Ellen. But the *Trib* was still filled with news of the other fire: "The Worst Disaster to ever hit Oakland." There were pictures, eye witness accounts from those who escaped, and countless other articles about fire fighting tactics, including the lack of communications between the various fire departments caused by some radio frequency problem. One article said they drew a line at the Claremont Hotel at the foot of the hills. An expert said if the fire had gotten past the hotel it would have hit two gas stations nearby causing a fire storm that would spread into the flatlands. With the Diablo Wind blasting like a bellows on the inferno, Oakland might have been completely wiped out. *Thanks to our brave fire fighters the city was saved.* I wondered if the owners of the homes that burned, or the families of the dead and injured, felt the same way. It was a matter of perspective I guess. My own problems seemed small in comparison, but they were my problems. It was a matter of perspective.

I'd have to stop by De Leures News stand on Broadway and pick up a copy of the *Press Democrat*, Santa Rosa's daily. Maybe there was something in there.

I finished by breakfast and left a healthy tip along with the *Trib* for the next customer. The cashier, who had been there since as long as I could remember, smiled and took my money with the comment,

"Too bad Flo's not here. We all miss her."

My pocket book *missed* her.

I stopped at the phone booth outside and called the Union Hall. Marta connected me to Gil without her usual sarcastic remarks. I told Gil about his car.

"It's okay," I said, "but its parked on the side of a road leading to a place called Stover's Winery, only its not really a winery, off Wall Road in the hills above Glen Ellen."

"Jesus, Smitty, what the hell you been up to...oh never mind. Don't worry about it. I'll call Triple A and have them pick it up. Wall Road?"

I was relieved. Gil was a good sport.

"Yeah," I'm really sorry..."

"Don't sweat it, brother."

"You're a real *mentsh,* Gil."

"Well, I guess that's good."

"It is, brother. You check on my car?"

"Oh shit. With the fire and everything things have been crazy around here. I just forgot all about it."

210

"Well, I'll check it out."

"Smitty. You okay?

"I'll live, Gil. Thanks for everything."

"Forget it brother. This local owes you."

I hung up and called Ted at his office, but was told he was working from his home. I dropped another quarter in and dialed his home number.

"Where the fuck you been?"

It seemed like Ted's customary greeting whenever I called him these days.

"Look Ted. I need you to drive me up to the Ashby BART. I left my car there two days ago."

"Why the fuck did you do that?"

"I can't tell you about it over the phone. Just come get me. I'll be in front of the Merritt Bakery."

""Goddamn it Smitty, I'm working. They got me doing a special feature on the fuckups by the fire departments. Seems no two fire departments operate on the same radio frequency, dumb bastards. "

"Just do this for me. It won't take you more than an hour."

"Well, okay. I've been worried about you comrade. Gabe called this morning and said you and your girl friend got into some heavy shit. I'll be there as soon as I can. You can fill me in with the details."

I went to a nearby bench and lit a cigarette. Ted lived in Alameda, but it wouldn't take him more than twenty minutes. I should have kept the newspaper, but instead I just sat there with my thoughts.

Ted must be really tight with Agent Feinberg for the FBI guy to call him and tell him what happened. Maybe Ted could convince him to tell me where Mei was. I had to remember to ask him. My mind drifted back to the early morning when we got to the apartment. Mei had seemed to know she wouldn't be coming with me. But how could she? It didn't add up. I could understand our rescue by the FBI guys. Berman was obviously following us. But that didn't explain the helicopter attack. I could still see Mei's smile as the flames lit up her face, as if she knew all along they were coming. But how could she? And why did she drag me to the ranch if she did know? Nothing made any sense.

Ted pulled up in front of the bench. I climbed into the passenger seat.

"Thanks," I said.

"You ought to thank me, you son of a bitch. Shit, I've been worried about you old buddy. "

"Why Ted, I didn't know you cared," I joked.

"Fuck you, Smitty. You're my best friend and I thought you got yourself killed," he said, looking straight ahead as we pulled out of the parking lot onto Park Street

I had always considered him my best friend, perhaps one of the only friends I had in the world, but I had never realized he felt the same way.

"Damn Ted, what's gotten into you. You never told me that."

"Oh hell, Smitty. My wife's taking sensitivity classes for her practice. Says they'll help her empathize with her patients.

"For Crissakes, she's a oral surgeon."

"Never mind. Anyway, she told me I should express my feelings more openly. So, I did. So what?"

"I'm really touched, pal. I really am."

"Fuck off, Smitty," he said.

He made a left on MacArthur, got onto 580 heading into Oakland, and then merged onto 24, taking the first exit onto MLK which would take us straight up to the Ashby BART station in Berkeley.

"You haven't asked me what happened over the past couple of days."

"Would you tell me if I did? Gabe said it was top secret,

hush hush shit; wouldn't tell me squat, so I don't expect you to either."

I was his best friend, or so he said, and I felt I was betraying our friendship by not telling him. But Ted was also a reporter, and if I told him I'd probably see it in print and the FBI would be picking me up and shipping me off to Leavenworth.

"Yeah, I guess not. Not now at least," I said.

We arrived at the station and Ted pulled into the parking lot. My car was still there. He pulled up to it and stopped.

"You're in luck. They didn't tow it; probably tied up with the fire. They called everyone in on that," Ted said.

"Yeah. Say Ted, my best friend."

"Listen, I can't do any more for you pal. I really got to get back to work."

"Yeah, I know," I said, opening the door. "Just one thing. You're tight with Agent Feinberg, right?"

"Gabe? " He nodded. "You could say that."

"Do me a favor and call him and see if you can find out where they took Mei-ling, would you? They took her into custody last night."

"Damn Smitty. You're really strung out behind that woman."

I couldn't look him in the eye. "I'm in love with her."

He laughed. "You've know this woman what; maybe two weeks? In love? I warned you about messing around with Asian women."

"You married one," I said defensively.

"I'm an expert. Well, I'll make a call. No guarantee he'll tell me."

"Thanks Ted. I owe you."

"You can buy me dinner tonight. The old lady's got one of her damn classes."

"Sure, I'll be happy to buy you dinner," I said, knowing he would probably stick me with the check anyway.

I watched as Ted drove out of the parking lot, heading back toward the freeway.

I drove up to the Enterprise car rental on Shattuck. The same guy who rented us the Honda was on duty. I explained to him that the car was burned up in the fire. He asked why I didn't contact them earlier and I gave him a lame excuse.

He looked up my contract.

"Isaac Smith ... 1990 Honda Accord. Well, you bought the insurance, so I guess your okay" he said with a look of disgust, like how dare I abandon his car in the Oakland Hills, as if it belonged to him.

I was in no mood to argue. I told him where they could find it, or what was left of it.

It was one-thirty in the afternoon and I was exhausted. I drove to the apartment on Lakeshore. The catastrophe of the fire didn't seem to have stopped people from their daily routines, Teeeeeeeeeeeeeeeeeeeeeeeeeeeeeeeeeeeeeeeeeeeeeeeeeeeeeeeeeehe park was filled with the usual joggers, young mothers and old folks, enjoying the warm day as if nothing had happened.

As for me, all I could think of was a couch and sleep. I found a parking spot near the steps to the apartment—a small miracle in itself. I stumbled up to the stairs, fumbled with my keys and finally entered the empty apartment. I collapsed onto the couch, and without even taking off my shoes, fell into a deep dreamless sleep.


I was jerked from the darkness by the phone ringing. The sun flowed brightly in through the window as it dropped down below the Oakland skyline. I glanced at the clock. It was six.

I answered: "So, we having dinner, or what," Ted said on the other end.

"Yeah, sure." My mind was switching back on. "Where?"

"How about Franciscos."

214

"By the airport?"

"You know any other Francisco's? They have Osso Bucco on the special tonight. I love their Osso Bucco."

"Okay, if you pick me up. Did you talk to agent Feinberg?"

"Yeah, I'll tell you all about it at dinner. I'll be by in about half an hour. Be ready."

I got up and went to the bathroom to take a shower wondering what Ted found out, knowing I shouldn't speculate, but couldn't help myself. I was afraid I had lost Mei-ling for good. I had to know why.

\* \* \*

# CHAPTER 38

I waited in front of the Apartment. Ted was on time as usual, like his whole life was ruled by a deadline. Or maybe he was just hungry.

The fog was starting to roll in from the west as I jumped into the front seat, and we set out for the I-80 heading toward the airport. We didn't talk much on the way.

Ted exited at Hegenberger Road and went west toward the airport until we came to Pardee—what I called the union four corners because the Teamsters hall took up the southwestern corner, the International Longshoremen's and Warehousemen's union filled the opposite corner, with the United Labor bank across from the Teamsters and Francesco's, the union Italian restaurant filling in the fourth corner.

I always figured Francisco's reMeined union because so many union officials eat there that if the union put up a picket line they'd probably go out of business. Ted parked in the sprawling parking lot in the rear.

We were greeted by Teresa Bargiacchi, the owner's middle aged daughter, who for all intents and purposes ran the place while her father, Dewey, puttered around in his vegetable garden along the side of the restaurant, and hobnobbed with the older customers. She had been raised in the business and knew it from top to bottom. Teresa acted as hostess, greeting people—many of whom she knew by first name—and escorted them to their seats. She was efficiency honed to a fine point. I had sat across from her at the negotiating table several times when the union contract was up for renewal. She was a fair minded, but tough negotiator.

She greeted us both by name. "It'll be about fifteen minutes unless you want to eat at the bar," she informed us.

I shrugged my shoulders, not caring one way or the other, but Ted insisted we wait for a table.

We went into the bar where Dino, the senior bartender was already pouring our drinks.

"Double Jack Daniels and a Stoli vodka martini with extra olives," he smiled, setting the drinks down in front of us, and then moved to the end of the bar and joined some other customers watching a baseball game on the large color TV in the corner of the lounge.

I took a sip of the bourbon. "So, what did Feinberg tell you."

Ted looked down into his drink, as if looking for an appropriate answer to my question.

"You sure you want to hear this now?" he finally said. "I don't think you're going to be happy with the answer, and there's no sense ruining your dinner."

I could feel a knot tightening in my stomach. "Too late for that. What did he tell you?"

He sipped his martini and popped an olive into his mouth, rolled it around for a moment, and then dropped the pit into his hand.

"Well, when he and his partner brought Mei-ling into the office, they were met by a couple of NSA guys. They expected someone from Immigrations and Gabe said he was surprised to see them there."

"NSA?"

"National Security Agency."

"What the fuck did they want with Mei-ling?" I was getting irritated. "What the fuck's going on?"

"Well, to make a long story short, your girl friend was taken to the Chinese Embassy."

"Was she handcuffed, or what?"

Ted took another sip of his martini. He avoided my eyes.

"According to Gabe, she went willingly."

"I don't understand," I said

"Well understand this, comrade. She flew out of San Francisco on Air China this morning." He put his hand on my shoulder and looked me in the eye. "She's gone, Smitty. You may as well face it."

"I don't fucking believe you," I said.

He let his hand slip from my shoulder and turned his eyes back on his martini.

"You don't have to believe me, Smitty. But that's what happened. Gabe said he checked Air China's passenger list and they confirmed she was on the flight."

I gulped down my drink. "I can't believe she left willingly without telling me. I just don't believe it..."

"I have your table ready, fellas." It was Teresa's smiling face.

I was on auto pilot for the rest of the evening. I ordered a bowl of minestrone soup. All I remember was Ted attacking the huge veal shank smothered in tomato sauce while I mechanically lifted my spoon to my face in a repetitive motion until my bowl was empty.

I paid the bill and declined Ted's offer to buy after-dinner drinks.

We didn't talk much on the way back to the apartment. Ted babbled about the fire and how the people who owned the houses that burned up were getting screwed by their insurance companies. I just looked out the window.

By the time Ted dropped me in front of the apartment, a low clinging fog was hovering over the lake. I started to open the door when Ted put his hand on my shoulder again. I turned to him, but couldn't make out his face in the darkness.

"Look pal. I know how you felt about Mei-ling. And she was a beautiful and bright woman; I'm not saying she didn't love you. But you have to understand. She had her own agenda. Damnit it, Smitty. I warned you about getting involved in this thing. Mei-ling is Chinese. For her, family and country are everything. And she's a Communist on top of that. There's nothing you could do to change that."

"I know you mean well, brother. But I don't care what you say. I may have only known her for a few weeks, but I believe she loves me. That's all."

I opened the door and started to get out. I heard Ted say as I stepped onto the sidewalk that he would check with me the next day. I stood on the street as Ted drove off, wondering if I was just trying to convince myself that he was wrong and that she really did love me.

The apartment was empty and cold. I didn't want to be there, but it was the only place I had to go. I left the lights out and made my way in the gloom to the cupboard where I found a half empty bottle of bourbon. I sat down at the kitchen table, poured myself a stiff shot and looked out over the city lights that rose above the low lying fog on the lake.

Then I noticed the blinking light on the answering machine. Maybe it was Mei-ling. My hopes rose as I pushed the playback button.

It was Dede, calling from Arkansas:

*Smitty. If you get this message, Chanel and I will be flying back to Oakland Friday. I hope everything is going well with you and your lady friend. I would appreciate it a lot if you could pick us up at the airport. We'll be flying in to Oakland at seven in the evening on United. Chanal can't wait to see her uncle Smitty. We both love you, Smitty. Hope to see you on Friday.*

The machine clicked off. I lit a cigarette and took a long drag. Dede's message should have cheered me up. It didn't.

\* \* \*

# CHAPTER 39

I couldn't sleep. Every time I closed my eyes the image of Mei-ling crowded my mind; sitting in her green dress with the embroidered dragon caressing her round breasts; the slits up the sides parted just enough to reveal her golden thighs; her shiny black hair gathered up on her head and held by a jade comb. I opened my eyes and then shut them again, only to have her face crawl back into my thoughts; her head thrown back in erotic pleasure; her black hair streaming down over her slender shoulders. Again I opened my eyes, then closed them, and again her face appeared; the flickering light from the flames reflected in her dark eyes, a tear rolling down her cheek, and a smile on her face.

My mind raced. Ted's words streamed in; she had her own agenda ... she went willingly. Chinese or not, I believed I knew Mei-ling. Even if she were a devoted Communist, I knew she was in love with me But if everything he said was true, then everything I knew about people from years of experience was shot to hell and I would never be able to trust my instincts again. Chinese, communist; it didn't matter. People are people.

I tossed and turned for what seemed like hours until I finally dropped off into a fitful sleep.

When I woke up it was after nine o'clock. The morning light streamed into the front window. I remembered there was no coffee, so I jumped into the shower, dressed and headed for the Merritt, only to stop half way there. I decided to go downtown to De Lauer's Newsstand instead where I could find a *Press Democrat*. I could grab a cup of coffee and Danish at one of the many small coffee shops. I went back and got my car.

I sat at the small table outside Davood's Coffee Shop on Twelfth Street with a cup of espresso and a sweet roll in front of me. I imagined I was in Europe. I opened the *Press Democrat* in search of any reference to the incident two night's before. I figured if there was anything it wouldn't have appeared in the issue the day before because it happened so late, or early in the a.m. depending on how you looked at it. Sure enough, an item on the local news page:

### STRANGE LIGHTS SEEN IN HILLS AROUND VALLEY OF THE MOON

Glen Ellen - Strange lights flashing in the hills overlooking Glen Ellen were reported to local authorities around 3 a.m. yesterday morning. There were no officers in the vicinity at the time.

Witness told the Press Democrat that they observed bright lights flashing on the east side of the hills, followed by a steady glow that disappeared after around an hour.

Old timers asked about the phenomenon said it was the spirits of Pomo Indian shamans performing ancient rituals in the sacred valley.

Authorities declined to comment.

I took a sip of the hot Espresso. So, that's all it was – a mysterious phenomenon. What could have been a Pulitzer Prize story about Chinese smugglers and a clandestine helicopter attack by a mysterious band of mercenaries right there in Sonoma County, California, was reduced to a small item in the *Press Democrat* and a nuisance complaint on the police blotter, because no one bothered to investigate. I laughed out loud. The woman sitting at the other outside table looked at me like I was nuts.

My next stop would be the Berkeley Marina. I wanted to check up on my boat. I had felt completely alone in the empty apartment. There were too many ghosts lingering there, and I longed to settle back in my maritime home where I could smell the gardenia blossom scent of Mei-ling in my bed. But first I stopped to see Johnny Wong. Out of everything that had happened over the past several days, bringing Johnny into it was the one thing I regretted most.

He greeted me at the door of his apartment like a long lost brother. I couldn't believe he was happy to see me. His leg was in a cast up to his waist and the bruises were still visible on his face. Turns out he was more concerned about my safety than I was about him. He asked about Mei-ling.

"She went back to China," I said

"I'm sorry, Smitty. I know how you felt about her. I warned you about getting mixed up in Chinatown. But I could see how you would fall in love with her. She was a knock out; classic Chinese beauty. It would never have worked though. You knew that."

I just stood there. It would never have worked.

"I'm sorry, Smitty. You want a drink? I have some JD in the cupboard." He started to limp back toward his kitchen.

"No thanks, Johnny. I just stopped by to see how you're doing."

"I'm cool, brother. I have a lot of sick leave on the books. And if they try to fire me, well, you won't let them, right?"

"Don't worry about it," I said, and helped him into a chair in front of the TV.


"Jesus, Smitty. I got some bad news for you," Skip said. "The Coast Guard found your boat—or what's left of it—beached between Santa Cruz and Monterey. It had been burnt down to the gunwales. I'm really sorry, Smitty."

More bad news. I now joined the hundreds of other people in Oakland who had lost their homes to fire.

"I checked with the Emeryville Marina and they said they'd contact your insurance company."

"Thanks," I said, and slowly walked back to my car. It seemed everything everything in my life had gone to shit.

I had no desire to go back to the apartment or go to my office. Too many questions. Too much to explain. I didn't want to talk to anyone. Instead I drove up University Avenue toward the campus, stopped at a liquor story and picked up a half pint of JD, and then made a left on Shattuck to Marin. From there it was a straight steep climb to GrizzlyPeak Boulevard and the entrance to Tilden Park.

For all the years I had lived in the East Bay I had never visited the sprawling park that stretched across the Berkeley Hills into Contra Costa County. It wasn't until Dede and her daughter, Chanal, came to live with me, and we went on picnics to the Little Farm. Chanal loved petting the farm animals.

I parked and walked to the corral. It was a weekday and there weren't many people. The cow came up to me. It was half lame and blind. I put out my hand and it licked me with its sandpaper tongue. Then I took out the half pint and took a long pull from the bottle.

"You and me, cow," I said, "Victims of our own existence; you locked up and me locked out. It seems life had dealt us both a rotten hand."

I decided to take a walk up to Jewel Lake. The sky was a deep Autumn blue and the sun was hot on my face. The path ran through a thick wooded area with a stream rushing along the side. I lit a cigarette, ignoring the no smoking signs, and took another hit from the half pint. As a walked the sadnessand self pity I had been feeling over the loss of Mei-ling began to turn to anger. The bitch! She had been playing me all along, I told myself. Disbelief, followed by sadness and then anger; it was text book stuff. But recognizing it didn't stop my anger from taking over, and I went with the flow, feeding on the anger like a healing elixir for the pain in my heart.

By the time I got to the Lake I had nearly convinced myself that I was better off that Mei-ling had dumped me and went back to China. At least there wouldn't be a chance of my running into her somewhere. I finished off the bottle and dumped it into a trash bin, and then headed back. My head was swimming from the bourbon and my brain went numb. The smells and sounds of the nature area were all that filled my senses. I was at peace, for the time being at least.

\* \* \*

# CHAPTER 40

I drove up Grand Ave and stopped at the Quarter Pounder for a hamburger and fries. The place was union, perhaps the only burger joint in America that was, and a hell of a lot better than McDonald's or Burger King. I bet they didn't have hamburgers in China. Mei-ling would miss that. I picked up a fifth of JD at a nearby liquor store and promised myself I'd quit drinking soon. I knew I was lying, but I had been lying to myself a lot in the past twenty-four hours. Shit, who was I fooling? I was still in love with Mei-ling, and the thought that she had left me and returned to China without a word became more painful then ever.

I got back to the apartment and poured a stiff drink. Then I went to the couch, kicked my shoes off, switched on the TV to keep me company, and started in on the burger and fries. They went well with the Jack Daniels.

The six o'clock news was on. They were reporting on the murder of a woman in North Oakland. The fire was yesterday's news despite the fact that the whole city had nearly burned up. It was worse than the Loma Prieta earthquake only two years before, but only worth a mention. Instead, the usual Oakland story about murder and mayhem. No motive or suspect in the killing according to the cops. Just some woman identified as Indira Benergee shot in her apartment.

Indy! It struck me like a brick. Why would anyone want to kill the sweet Indian college professor? It was senseless until a horrifying thought hit me. With Mei-ling in China, the only other people in the world who knew about the stolen pandas were the Chinese government and a few mucky-mucks in the State Department. They had wanted it to reMein a secret at all costs. Rick was going to blow me away because of that knowledge, and only the unexpected appearance of Agent Feinberg and Ted saved my ass. Shit, he was even willing to kill Mei-ling when she attempted to come to my rescue They were erasing any trace of anyone who may know about their state secret. Rick could be gunning for me at that moment.

I was terrified. I got up and double checked the locks on the door. It was a feeble act, but I didn't know what else to do. I wished Mei-ling was there. She'd know. But she was five thousand miles away, and for all I knew, didn't give a shit, otherwise she would never have left. That thought sent me into a new funk. I returned to the couch and filled my glass with Tennessee's finest.

I tried to concentrate on the TV, but my fear overwhelmed me. I had to do something, but what? I could call Agent Feinberg; ask to be taken into protective custody; warn them that a Chinese assassin was on the loss. But I'd have to explain why I thought I was being hunted down, and I promised Mei-ling I wouldn't tell anyone about the pandas. There were few things that were sacred to me, and my word was one of them. I wouldn't break my promise to Mei-ling, even if she had broken my heart. I had hoped that they had forgotten all about me, but with Indira's murder I knew I'd be next.

The last thing I remember before passing out was the weatherman saying a low fog was expected to roll in later that night.


There was a ringing in my head coming from far off. I wanted to turn it off, but I couldn't find it. Then my eyes opened. The Johnny Carson show was on, but the ringing was coming from the front door. It soon turned to knocking; not loud, but determined. I went the door and stuck my eye on the peep hole, something I never did since the security gate usually keep unwanted people out. But the gate wasn't always closed all the way even though there was a sign telling people to make sure it was locked.

The face in front of the door was shaded by the outside light behind him. I had meant to put a new bulb in the alcove lamp, but never had. I kept looking without breathing until whoever it was stepped back into the light. It was Rick, standing there with his hands in the pockets of his short leather jacket and Ray-Ban shades covering his eyes even though it was the middle of the night. Shit, everyone in the world was either asleep or watching Johnny Carson, but not Rick. He had returned to finish the job.

"Open the door, Smitty. I know you're in there," I heard him through the thin door.

I wasn't about to open it and let him shoot me in the face. If he was going to kill me he'd have to work for it, and I hoped he wouldn't want to make a lot of noise by kicking the door down.

I made my way to the back door that opened on to a small

deck and narrow corridor between my apartment and the one next to it. There was just enough room on the deck for the communal garbage can. The corridor led to the front of the building. I was in such a panic to get out of the apartment that I had forgotten to put my shoes on, but I wasn't about to go back for them. It was just as well. I moved silently down the corridor in my stocking feet. When I reached the end I stopped and peaked out onto the patio entrance of the apartment building. A cold wind was blowing in across the lake and I could feel the fog hit my flushed face like a slap. I hadn't stopped to get a coat and a chill ran through me, although it was as much fear as it was the change in the weather.

There was no sign of Rick. He must have still been in the alcove in front of the apartment's front door. The gate leading to the stairs leading down to Lakeshore Boulevard was wide open, giving me an easy escape route. I wouldn't make any noise in my socking feet, so I made a run for it. But when I hit the gate I kicked something and there was a loud yowl followed by a hissing. My neighbor's goddamn black cat. There was nothing left but to get to the stairs and get down to the street before Rick figured out what was happening.

I glanced up just before my head dropped below the cement patio and saw Rick step out from the alcove.

"Smitty, is that you? Where you going?!"

I grabbed the railing to keep myself from tripping as my feet moved as fast as they could down the steep stairs. I heard heavy foot steps behind me, echoing in the stair well as I hit the street level.

"Smitty, wait a second!"

The street light glared through the haze and I could barely make out the necklace of lights around the lake. The fog made everything obscure. There was no traffic. I bolted across the street into the park and ducked behind a tree, trying to catch my breath. When I peeked out, Rick was still on the other side of Lakeshore. He pushed up his Ray-Bans and looked around. Then he started across the street. I panicked and started running again.

"Smitty!" I could hear him shout after me.

I was running blindly. I could feel the wetness of the damp grass mixed with Goose shit soak through my socks. Where was a cop when I needed one? I pictured the next day's headline in my head: *Unidentified Man Found Shot To Death At Lake Merritt.* My buddy, Ted, would probably write the story.

I kept running with no idea where I was going. I could sense Rick bearing down on me. He was younger by at least ten years. My legs felt like lead, but I forced them to move, until suddenly the screeching of irate geese and the loud flapping of wings filled my head. I could see the shadows of dozens of birds rising in front of me, and then my face smacked into a solid feathered body, heard the loud  protesting honk of a goose, and found myself hitting the wet ground.

Before I could recover, Rick was on me. I rolled over and stared up into the sunglasses staring down at me. Rick was breathing heavily. God damned geese. I could see the flock that had been my downfall settling not far from where I had run into them. I just didn't give a shit anymore. Mei was gone. Everything was fucked up. I was ready for the bullet. But ...

"Damnit, Smitty. Why the fuck you run from me?" he panted.

He had his hands in his jacked pockets and I wondered why he didn't just pull out his gun and shoot me on the spot. But he didn't, and for a moment I wished he would hand me his pistol so I could kill of couple of the damn geese. But, instead, he pulled his hands out from his jacket and showed me they were empty.

"You're not going to kill me?"

"Well" he smiled, "I can't say the thought hadn't crossed my mind after you took off. But no, I'm not going to shoot you."

He put out his hand in a gesture to help me to my feet. I took it and he pulled me up.

"Come on, man. Let's get back to your apartment where it's warm. What do you say?"

"So you can shoot me there?"

"Smitty, I told you I'm not going to kill you."

I didn't know whether to believe him or not, but what the hell. Murdered in the park, or in the apartment; it made no difference. He took my arm, like he was helping his feeble grandfather, and we headed silently back up to Lakeshore and across the street to the apartment building.


"You have some tea?" Rick asked.

"No." I said, pulling off my wet socks and rubbing my feet with a towel. If I had to die, I'd die with dry feet.

"No tea? Coffee?"

"No," I said again.

"Well, Okay." He sat down on the chair across from me at the kitchen table. "Why did you think I came to kill you, man?"

I looked up at him. "You killed that poor Indian girl friend of Mei-ling's. She probably didn't know anything. Why did you do that?"

Rick didn't respond.

"So, why shouldn't I assume your going to kill me? You tried before."

I threw the towel on the floor. My shirt and pants were wet and I was shivering. I wanted to take a hot shower and never get out. Stupid, considering I was probably going to be dead anyway.

"You ought to get out of those wet clothes or you'll get sick," Rick said. "You sure you don't have any tea?"

He got up and looked around the room, spotting the

bottle of Jack Daniels on the coffee table next to my half eaten hamburger. He glanced at the Johnny Carson show which was still on.

"Jay Leno still guest hosting I see," he remarked, and then came back into the kitchen, took the tea kettle that sat on the stove, filled it with water and put it back on a burner..

"Some whiskey and hot water; just the thing," he said. "You go change into some dry clothes."

It all seemed wrong. Why was he being so nice to me? But I was cold and wet and didn't argue. I was too tired to care any more. If he was going to let me get comfortable and give me a drink before he killed me; well, so be it. I picked up the towel and went to Dede's bedroom where I still had some clothes

"Keep the door open," Rick called after me.

I stripped, dried myself off and slipped into some cotton sweat pants and matching sweat shirt, that Dede had bought for me. I felt oddly self conscious knowing Rick was watching.

"Well, that's better.," Rick said as I came out of the bedroom. "Now for that hot toddy."

"Forget the hot water. I'll just take a glass of whiskey."

"Suit yourself," Rick said. "But I recommend a toddy to prevent a cold."

"Can't make a Toddy."

"Why's that?"

"No honey. No lemon," I said, like it was my professional duty to tell him the recipe for a hot toddy.

I went into the attached living room, turned off the TV and sat heavily onto the couch. I poured the JD into my empty glass and lit up a Lucky from the pack that I had left on the coffee table.

"So, what's all this about?" I asked accusingly. "If you're not going to kill me, what the hell are you doing here?"

Rick dragged a kitchen chair into the living room and straddled it in front of me.

"Smitty, you're a suspicious guy. I came to tell you about Mei-ling."

"I already know. She went back to China, and according to what I hear, she went willingly. What else is there to know?"

"And you think she's some kind of Chinese cunt for running out on you like that."

"Well?"

Rick looked at me and slowly shook his head.
"Damn, Smitty. The woman was ready to give up her life in order to save yours. And believe me, I would have shot the two of you if that FBI prick didn't show up. Look, Smitty. I like you, but you're a real assshole if you think Mei-ling didn't love you."

"How do you mean? She ran out on me without a word." I said.

"Well, if I have to spell it out for you; Mei-ling made a deal. She had contacted us from Glen Ellen. She said she'd tell us where the pandas were being kept on one condition; that you be left alone. The head of security, my boss, conferred with his superiors and they agreed to her demand for your safety, but she would have to return to China. That was the deal, Smitty. That's the only reason you're still alive."

I was stuck. If what he said was true, and there was no reason not to believe him, then I was a real *shmuck*.

"Hell, if we were going to kill you, we would have done it at the ranch. Yes, we knew you and Mei-ling were there."

"How did you know that?"

"When she talked to us she said she was going to take a shot at the place in case we couldn't arrange something on short notice. She was worried they'd be moving the pandas at any time. So, you see, with those fucking mercenaries your State Department rounded up for us, you and Mei-ling were lucky to get out of there alive."

"Even with the FBI guys there?"

"We didn't know about them until later."

"And what about the Indian girl?"

Rick got up from the chair. "I don't know anything about that. I told you, I could get in a lot of hot water for telling you what I told you."

With that, Rick got up. "You take care of yourself, Smitty. I hope you don't catch cold." And he was gone.

I hoped it was the last time I would ever see him.

* * *

# CHAPTER 41

I didn't sleep the rest if the night. I just sat on the couch, staring into the darkness, dozing now and then, only to be jarred awake by my thoughts

Rick's visit seemed like a dream. But it was real, and he had no reason to lie to me and he had every reason to kill me. But now it didn't seem to matter other than the satisfaction of knowing Mei-ling *did* love me—if what Rick told me could be believed—and that I had been right about her all along. But the fact was that Mei-ling was gone; out of my life forever, and there was nothing I could do about it.

I thought of poor Indy, the pretty Indian woman, killed in her own apartment. Rick said he didn't know anything about it, but someone must have because she was dead. I suddenly feared for Dede and Chanel. Would they be targets just because they knew me? And what about Ted? Would they take a chance that he knew their big secret and would put it in the newspaper?

Fucking pandas. Who would have believed that the loss

of some fucking baby bears—cute as they were—could cause so much violence, just because the Chinese Government was afraid of losing face in the eyes of the world? And the fact was, I had never actually seen the pandas. It was all total insanity.

The morning light started filtering into the apartment's windows. I got up from the couch and walked over to the kitchen table. The fog that had hovered over the lake was gone, leaving a grey dawn.

I put on my shoes and went out into the morning. The black cat, that had tripped me up, was standing at my neighbor's door howling to get in.

I walked down the stairs to the street and crossed over to the lake. Hundreds of Canadian geese were munching away on the grass. I wondered which of the bastards had plowed into my face the night before. I could still feel the welt it left on my cheek.

It wasn't more than six o'clock. I decided to take a long walk around the lake and come back to the Merritt for coffee.

There were a few early morning joggers, getting in their exercise before going to work. I was impressed by they're discipline. I knew I could never do it. I doubted if I could even jog. How did I run from Rick, until the fuckig goose brought me down, was a mystery. Fear I suppose. I breathed in the cool morning air and immediately started coughing. Damn cigarettes.

I sat on a bench half way around the lake near the boat house and lit up. I should warn Ted that he may be a target. He could call his buddy in the FBI. There was nothing else I could do.

I should call Dede, explain the situation and tell her to cancel her flight and stay in Arkansas for a while. But I knew Dede, and I knew she wouldn't do that. Dede wasn't afraid of anything, so it was my responsibility to protect her and Chanel.

It was too much to digest without my morning coffee, so I snuffed out my cigarette and walked the rest of the way around the lake until I reached the Merritt. I bought the morning

*Tribune* and went to my usual spot at the counter. The waitress, a young white woman I had never seen before, poured a cup of coffee.

"Are you ready to order?" she asked.

"Just the coffee," I answered.

I glanced at the paper and an article of the front page immediately caught my attention:

### Indian Man Arrested At
### Airport In Connection With
### UC Prof Murder

*by Ted Harlan*
*Tribune Crime reporter*

A citizen of Bangelor, India was arrested last night in connection with the murder of University of California professor, Indira Banerjii, last night by Oakland Police. He was trying to catch a flight back to India at the Oakland Airport at the time of the arrest.

The man was identified by police as the brother of Indira Banerjii who was found shot to death two nights ago in her apartment in North Oakland.

According to police sources, the man, Ravi Benargii, confessed to having killed his sister because she had dishonored her family.

Ms. Banerjii had come from India over six years ago and became a full professor in South-East Asia studies at UC Berkeley two years later.

Police called the incident very rare. While honor killings are common place in countries like Turkey, India and Pakistan, Professor Franklyn Rabinski, head of the Asian Studies Department at UC, and a friend of Ms. Banerjii told the Tribune it has only been recently that such killings have appeared in the United States.

Rabinski credited the increase to the rapidly growing numbers of East Asians coming to the U.S. for work in the computer industry.

"Honor killings occur when a member of a family or social group believe that the victim has brought dishonor upon the family or community. They are directed mostly against women and girls," Rabinski explained "These can include; marrying without the family's permission, promiscious behavior, homosexual behavior, and a list of other offenses that supposedly would bring dishonor on the family," he explained, adding that he could attest that Banerjii was not a homosexual, but would not elaborate.

"I always thought that she was escaping from something in India, but she would never talk about it," Rabinski said.

Ravi Banerjii is being held at Santa Rita County Jail until a preliminary hearing scheduled for this morning in Superior Court.

"That son of a bitch Rabinski seduced Indy too," I thought out loud. No wonder she and Mei became good friends.

If the story was true Indy's death had nothing to do with Rick or the Chinese Consulate. Rick wasn't bullshitting me after all, and that meant Ted and Dede were safe.

It was a big load off my mind. I stuck my hand in my coat pocket for a cigarette and came out with a slip of note paper. It was from the Jack London Inn.

My Dearest Isaac,

No matter what happens, I want you to know I love you very much. But I must return to China if all goes as planned tonight. I am leaving, not because I don't love you, but because it is the only way I can protect you. But I promise that our paths have not reached an end. I don't know when, but somehow I will return to you. my love.

Mei

It was true, what Rick had told me. I suddenly felt guilty for having doubted her love. Yes, I was an asshole. But what she had done—returning to China—was for me. She had given up everything she had known for the past twenty years to save my wothless butt.

Suddenly I was very hungry. "Hey, sweetheart," I called to the young waitress.

She was an attractive asian girl, maybe twenty years old. She gave me a big smile.

"Have you changed your mind, sir?"

"Yes," I said and ordered a waffle, bacon fried eggs and rye toast. Dark.

I took another drink of coffee and she filled my cup up. *She's a good waitress,* I thought to myself.

I opened the paper to kill the time until my breakfast came up. I saw one of the cooks grab my ticket and pour the waffle mix in one smooth motion. Then I glanced back at the paper and notice a small item in the World section.

## China Executes Four
## Red Army Officers

BEIJING - Four high ranking officers of the Red Army in charge of the People's Natural Resource were executed earlier this week, the official Xinhua News Service reported.

The men were charged with corruption and treason. Authorities in Szechuan province, said dozen of arrests have taken place over the past several weeks as part of what authorities called a breakdown in authority at the Wolong National Nature Reserve where the world's only population of Panda Bears are protected.

Yu Yuan, Cultural Minister in charge of National Resources, said that the gang was broken up before any damage had been done, and that all the Pandas on the reserve had been accounted for.

Attempts by Western reporters to learn more about the situation were unsuccessful.

And that's all they'd find out, I thought out loud. As far as I knew I was the only person outside official government agencies that knew the truth about the lapse in Chinese security, and I would never tell. I had made a promise to Mei-ling, and when a man gives his word, he keeps it.

Sure, Mei-ling was gone from my life, but she promised she would return. Maybe she would. Maybe not. No matter. I don't think I ever loved a woman as much as I loved the Chinese lady in the Green dress.

# The End

*Don't miss the exciting
sequel to Promise To A Dead Man as Mei-ling must
find a way to escape Red China and return to her lover
who is being hunted by assassins.*

Promise To A Dead Man

# The Author

*L.Z. Smith has lived in the San Francisco Bay Area for over 30 years.*

*He has primarily worked as a political and labor journalist, with occasional side trips into fiction writing and independent film scripting.*

*He boasts three beautiful daughters, two beautiful step daughters, four beautiful grandchildren, an ancient but seaworthy sailboat, and a very indulgent woman.*

*His previous book, The Bartender Ran Last, was the first in this series of Isaac Smith Mysteries.*

L.Z. Smith